MICHAEL INNES

SHEIKS
AND
ADDERS

PENGUIN BOOKS

W9-AFD-577

Penguin Books Ltd, Harmondsworth, Middlesex, England
Penguin Books, 40 West 23rd Street, New York, New York 10010, U.S.A.
Penguin Books Australia Ltd, Ringwood, Victoria, Australia
Penguin Books Canada Ltd, 2801 John Street, Markham, Ontario, Canada L3R 1B4
Penguin Books (N.Z.) Ltd, 182–190 Wairau Road, Auckland 10, New Zealand

First published in Great Britain by Victor Gollancz Ltd 1982
First published in the United States of America by Dodd, Mead and Company 1982
Published in Penguin Books 1983

Made and printed in Great Britain by
Cox & Wyman Ltd, Reading
Set in Linotron Sabon by
Rowland Phototypesetting Ltd,
Bury St Edmunds, Suffolk

I

John Appleby, although a knight, would not have thought of himself as one likely to turn knight-errant. And certainly not in his years of retirement, during which a sedentary habit had been gaining on him. This became a topic of conversation one afternoon, when a new neighbour had paid a call on the Applebys. His name was McIlwraith, and he too had recently retired – after, it seemed, a variegated academic career. As a young man he had put in a long spell as Professor of Romance Languages in Tehran or some such place, and during this odd assignment had built himself up as a somewhat old-fashioned polyglot philologist, producing a number of dictionaries of one sort and another – all of them single-handed in the heroic manner exemplified by Dr Johnson. Back in an English university, he had become up-to-date again in some fashionable field of linguistics. But his talk turned out to be still distinctly on the lexicographical side.

'How do I occupy my time?' Appleby repeated. (For Professor McIlwraith was a sharply inquiring man.) 'Well, I've learnt to prune Judith's roses to her satisfaction –'

'Nearly always to her satisfaction,' Judith Appleby interrupted. 'And I'm fairly pernickety, I suppose. John is careful, but takes his time.'

'I'd guess you were exigent, Lady Appleby,' Professor McIlwraith said. 'But are you Scotch as well?'

'Certainly not.' It was plain that Judith disapproved of this idea. 'What should put such a thing in your head?'

'"Pernickety" is a word I heard most frequently when I

was a boy in Aberdeen. It belongs to an interesting group of Scots words which the English owe to literary men of Scottish nationality active down here in the later nineteenth century.'

'How very interesting,' Judith said politely. 'But John wants to tell you all the other things he does.'

'The rough,' Appleby said. 'I may modestly claim that I do the rough. The aged Hoobin, a gardener long in the service of my wife's family, becomes more and more deeply what he calls a perusing man. His studies, which occupy virtually his entire working day, take place in the potting shed. Hoobin is a true scholar.'

'Dear me – how very gratifying. And what is Hoobin's particular field of scholarship? As a whole, the labouring classes nowadays lack the spirit of self-improvement, do they not?'

'I am afraid so. And Hoobin's application is to the *Daily Mirror*. His nephew Solo, on the other hand, whom we retain to assist the good old man, as yet lacks the equipment to peruse anything. It may be an almost entirely fortunate circumstance. What is regrettable about Solo is that he is hardly ever awake. Did we not know him to have been bred on the property, we might suppose him to have come into the world at Mr Wardle's Dingley Dell.'

'Is Solo actually a fat boy?'

'He is almost a skeleton, although Judith is constantly giving instructions that he be plumped out.'

'It seems unfortunate, Sir John, that you should have to exert yourself out of doors in default of the proper services of this uncle and nephew.'

'It's healthy,' Judith said.

'That is what I have to bear in mind.' Appleby offered his guest a serious and indeed solemn look. 'Of course, pruning the roses is prickly rather than physically oppressive labour, and I take care never to do it from my wheelchair. But I also mow the grass, and as there's rather a lot of that I'm afraid it's on a sit-down affair called a rider. I trundle along on it, feeling rather like an American playing golf. However, I do at least run the errands on my own feet.'

'Now, just what is an errand?' Professor McIlwraith asked (perhaps momentarily forgetting that he was not conducting a seminar – or perhaps by way of getting back to ground on which he could be sure he wasn't being made fun of). 'Would it be a matter of bearing an instruction or commission on some other person's behalf?'

'It would be shopping, chiefly.'

'Ah, yes!' Professor McIlwraith was delighted. 'Do you know that in my native city –'

'Aberdeen?' Judith asked encouragingly.

'Yes, Aberdeen. When I was a boy, and shopping was in question, I would be sent out "to do the messages". And a message boy didn't carry messages; he delivered goods. "Have you any messages?" meant essentially "Is there anything you want me to buy?" I doubt whether in England the question would be understood in that sense. Unless, of course, in the presence of some strong contextual suggestion. But quite as interesting as "errand", I think you will agree, is "errant". Originally one is so described simply if one is travelling or wandering. But eventually the word comes to imply something like "deviating from the straight and narrow path", and thus acquires an opprobrious connotation.'

'So that if one is errant nowadays,' Appleby said, 'one is aberrant.'

'Excellently put, Sir John. How fascinating those very simple aspects of semasiology can be.'

'Yes, indeed.' Judith had to supply the civil acquiescence that her husband had been a little slow in coming forward with. 'But consider knight-errants – or is it knights-errant? They didn't have a straight and narrow path to deviate from. They'd simply be meandering through forests and places, and something would bump up against them and they'd cope with it.'

'Not a bad sort of life,' Appleby said. 'Full of surprises and calls for quick action.'

'Well, yes.' Judith glanced curiously at her husband, perhaps reflecting that the pruning of rose bushes seldom called for quite that. And then Professor McIlwraith was off again.

'"Meander" is notable, is it not?' he asked. 'The river is, of course, in Phrygia – or Anatolia, as we might now say. The use of the word attributively occurs in Spanish, Portuguese and Italian, and in English is first definitely so employed by Sir Thomas Browne.'

'What about "maunder"?' Appleby inquired – apparently without malicious intention. 'Maundering is a kind of verbal meandering. Perhaps there was a River Maunder in Phrygia too.'

'I think not,' Professor McIlwraith said comfortably. '"Maunder" is probably purely imitative in etymology, like "shoo" and "boohoo".'

'And "fee-faw-fum",' Appleby offered gravely.

'Ah!' The Applebys' guest appeared to be much struck by this. '"Fee-faw-fum",' he repeated appreciatively. 'Yes, indeed. "Fee-faw-fum". Do you know? I am inclined to hazard that "fee-faw-fum" defies philology.'

'It's a kind of gloat,' Judith said. 'A malign ejaculation.'

'Admirably expressed, Lady Appleby.' Professor McIlwraith got to his feet, and was suddenly a polite old gentleman aware that the time allotted to a first and formal call was over. 'A most delightful chat,' he said. 'We have shared enthusiasms, have we not? We must indulge them from time to time.'

Sir John Appleby conducted Professor McIlwraith down the drive of Long Dream Manor, and detained him for some further minutes in order to inquire into various points of comfort in his new house. Then he shook hands and retraced his steps – a shade gloomily, as may befall a man conscious of being so *désœuvré* as to have filled in time talking a good deal of nonsense. A detour took him past the potting shed, where he suffered the further discomfiture of observing Hoobin deeply involved in his habitual labour. But Hoobin lowered his paper as his employer approached.

'Would that ha' been the new furriner?' he asked.

'Yes, indeed, Hoobin. A Professor McIlwraith. Another very learned man.'

'Had he any call?'

'Had he what?'

'Any call to call. Furriners ha' no business to make themselves known unbid.'

'We mustn't be too punctilious, Hoobin. And I have probably been at fault myself. Professor McIlwraith is known to be a widower, and no doubt I ought to have taken some initiative in the matter myself.'

'It should be a long time afore we take account of furriners.'

'Possibly so.' Appleby found this xenophobe note depressing. 'Where' – he asked by way of changing the subject – 'is Solo?'

'The dratted boy's asleep again.'

'And I used to wonder,' Appleby said darkly, 'why this place is called Long Dream.'

The aged Hoobin, who perhaps made nothing of this remark, returned to his paper, and Appleby returned to the house still not in a very genial mood.

'An accession to our neighbourhood, the learned McIlwraith,' he said to his wife. 'A most stimulating chap, and with a breadth of view fully equal to that of dear old Mrs Mince, or Admiral Havering, or even the Birch-Blackies themselves.'

'I'm not sure there isn't a little more to Professor McIlwraith than appears. If he's not exactly a dark horse, at least he's a piebald one. And in any case, John dear, don't be supercilious.'

'I'm sorry. Admirable people, all of them. And I'm not a bit bored, you know – not a bit.'

'Why should you be? You have that knack. I believe

9

"knack" must be of what is called echoic origin. Don't you?'

'Who's mocking that erudite character now? But what knack are you talking about?'

'The knack of being bumped into when meandering, of course. It keeps on happening. So don't despair.'

Nothing of all this can have been lingering in Appleby's mind a few days later as he drove home from a duty visit to an octogenarian female relative in Bath. Bath, thought of as a 'distant kingdom' by the Wessex rustics of Thomas Hardy, was quite a considerable distance from Long Dream too, and Appleby had in consequence started his return journey at an early hour in the afternoon. So he had arrived on familiar ground, and was in fact passing through the successive rural centres of King's Yatter and Abbot's Yatter, while still having abundant time in hand before dinner. Indeed, he had only to traverse the region known as Boxer's Bottom, and thence ascend to the brow of Sleep's Hill, to command with binoculars (if prompted to do such a thing) the ancient stone roof and obsolete brick chimney-stacks of his own dwelling.

Meanwhile, on his left hand lay the Forest of Drool. It couldn't really be a forest, but it was certainly a very considerable tract of woodland territory. And it so happened that Appleby, although he had walked over most of this countryside at one time or another, had never penetrated this stretch of it. Now here it lay, dark and mysterious if one chose to think it so, but with numerous broad ridings and scattered glades expansed beneath a cloudless June sky. Here and there, moreover, some local authority, bowing before the spirit of the age, had put up sundry small signposts of a positively inviting sort. Most of these said 'Footpath', and a few – by way of variety – said 'Bridleway'. Those saying 'Footpath' carried in addition a schematic representation of a couple of men walking, and those saying 'Bridleway' similarly displayed a single man leading a horse – a thoughtful provision,

Appleby supposed, for pedestrians from the Emirates of the Middle East, or perhaps merely for that increasing proportion of the inhabitants of these islands to whom – as to Solo – it had not occurred to learn to read.

Miss Appleby of Bath had not been inspiriting; in this regard, indeed, she might be estimated as rating very much with dear old Mrs Mince of Long Dream. But Mrs Mince at least didn't keep a parrot. With Miss Appleby's parrot Appleby had been obliged to converse. And since the creature was held to be a tropical bird, requiring for its health a very warm temperature indeed, visiting Miss Appleby had been a decidedly stuffy and sticky experience. Appleby felt he needed fresh air – more of it, even, than was blowing through the open windows of the old Rover as he drove. He also felt that he wanted to stretch his legs. And it was thus that he presently found himself drawn up in a parking place and scrambling from the car.

Enter those enchanted woods, you who dare . . . There was no reason to suppose the rather grandly named Forest of Drool to harbour much in the way of enchantment, nor did Appleby feel he had to dare anything as he negotiated a stile and plunged within its shades. He wasn't even risking being taxed with trespass: behaviour which a retired policeman should particularly seek to avoid. There was a perfectly well-defined footpath before him, and above his head one of the little signposts made the point, as it were, over again – like a bath mat that says 'bath mat' in case you should mistake it for a drawing-room rug. Nevertheless Appleby did faintly feel that he was being adventurous, and the absurdity of this sensation actually occupied his mind for the first hundred yards or so of his stroll. As a small boy, he supposed, something had happened to him in a wood. He might have come upon some wild creature horrifyingly caught in a trap. A fox might have startled him. A nasty old man might have made faces at him. An equally nasty old woman might have begged the little gentleman to spare a copper, but at the same time have betrayed the fact that she was a witch. Or perhaps he had played exciting Robin Hood games with rather bigger boys, and been more scared of the Sheriff of Nottingham and his men than he had cared to admit. Very probably he had been told that, if captured, he would be hanged.

These were idle fancies. Yet it is true, Appleby told himself, that one can suddenly be aware of experiencing – although never for more than the briefest moment – a sharp recrudescence of sensation which one knows perfectly well to have attached to some specific occasion years ago. One tries to identify the occasion, but the elusive memory vanishes, leaving the mind a total blank. If Appleby was interested in this phenomenon, it was perhaps because the practice of criminal investigation turns up something similar from time to time. A tiny signal arrives from the region of buried memory; catch it and hold it and you have solved your mystery. But too often it dissolves away again in the instant that you put out your hand. This, however, was past history so far as he was now concerned. Scotland Yard had become, for all practical purposes, as far removed from him as was the Taj Mahal. He was an elderly individual taking a late afternoon stroll amid sylvan scenes remote from any sort of mystification whatever. He was certainly meandering – the word came back to him from that pedantic old professor's visit – but it had been absurd for Judith to say that, when so employed, he had the knack of persuading untoward situations to come bumping into him. His business now was to note with satisfaction the various appearances of external nature in evidence.

But what next caught his attention was the handiwork of man. It was a square board nailed to a tree, and lettered in a much bolder fashion than had been the signposts of his first observation. And whereas they had invited carefree pedestrianism in the Forest of Drool, this one was distinctly forbidding. It read simply:

ADDERS
KEEP OUT

Appleby received this injunction with displeasure. He was offended, in the first place, by the irrationality of being bidden to keep out of something he must already be near the middle of. It was of course possible that the present location of the notice was a product of the same species of juvenile rustic humour as frequently occasioned the turning of signposts the wrong way round. Or conceivably Appleby had arrived at a point, not otherwise demarcated, at which one landowner's territory gave place to that of another more nervously disposed. Or the assertion might be quite untrue, like the ones saying 'Trespassers will be prosecuted', but more effective than that hackneyed kind, all the same. An authentic proliferation of adders was surely improbable. However all this might be, the mandatory phraseology of the notice was objectionable. Appleby had lately visited a Cambridge college, and been edified by a placard saying, 'It is earnestly desired by the Master and Fellows that perambulators be not perambulated on the grass'. He now saw no reason to be deterred from further perambulating himself in the Forest of Drool.

So he walked on in restored equanimity. There was much to observe. The beech trees had the curious form sometimes to be remarked of them, thrusting up out of the ground like a bunch of pencils or like so many fingers held tightly together as if in an act of prayer. Midsummer Day was only round the corner; primroses had given way to bluebells, and now the bluebells were yielding to campion and brier rose. There was a faint murmur in the air that spoke of a vigorous if invisible insect life, and the feathered songsters of the grove their various notes supplied. The wise thrush sang his song twice over; the woodland linnet – also no mean preacher – dispensed his unbookish wisdom as he flew; Appleby sat down for a few minutes on a tree trunk and was entertained alike by the various birds and their familiar poetic associations; then he glanced at his watch and decided he must return to the Rover. Still just ahead of him, however, the path took a turn round a hazel thicket and vanished. What happened round this bosky corner? The answer, almost certainly, was 'Nothing at all'; the Forest of Drool simply went on as forests do. Nevertheless Appleby felt that he might as well walk on and see. There might be an interesting little vista down a long straight riding. He might even come upon a badger poking a misdoubting snout into sunlight. There was everything to be said for continuing to advance another hundred yards or so.

So Appleby penetrated a little further. What he came upon almost at once was something much less interesting than badgers. It was a Range Rover, halted on a broad green riding which here cut across his own path at right-angles. Beside it stood a tall lean man in an attitude suggesting a momentary pause from labour. But not a labouring man in the accepted sense of the term, since something not readily definable about him proclaimed his adherence to the academic, or at least the investigating, class of society. He could very well have passed the time of day, Appleby thought, with the Applebys' new neighbour, Professor McIlwraith. Appleby ventured to pass the time of day himself.

'Good afternoon,' he said – and as he did so observed that the owner of the Range Rover was holding in his hand a piece of apparatus not readily to be identified. It was a long light pole, equipped at one end with what seemed to be a trigger-like device operating along a slender metal rod. At the other end there dangled what seemed to be a small wire loop or noose. It wasn't a fishing-rod, nor was it a butterfly-net, but it did belong to that order of contrivance. Appleby had distinguished so much when his glance went to the vehicle, which proved to bear a neatly lettered inscription. This read:

OXFORD UNIVERSITY INSTITUTE OF
ADVANCED HERPETOLOGY

'Dear me!' he said. 'May I ask, sir, if you are engaged in eradicating the adders?'

'Ah, the adders! No doubt you have seen that absurd notice. Not that there are *no* adders. Indeed, I have seen several today, and hope to get hold of a few. But it cannot be said that I am positively engaged on a venation of vipers, sir. I am simply collecting grass snakes. And when I conclude my foray tomorrow I am confident I shall have about a hundred of them.'

'But surely grass snakes are quite harmless?'

'Oh, entirely so – although few will be persuaded of the fact. I am not, I fear, performing any kind of public service, but simply stocking up for certain large-scale experiments at our Institute. It is quite a new concern, you know.'

'I am most interested to hear of it,' Appleby said politely. 'And it's being of recent foundation must excuse my not having heard of it at Oxford before.'

'Our fame is all to earn, my dear sir. And there were those who objected to the innovation on the score that at Oxford there are abundant snakes in the grass already.'

Appleby received this donnish witticism with appropriate subdued amusement, and lingered for a few moments in further talk. He rather hoped to be treated to a glimpse of this devoted scientist in action. But that didn't happen. Perhaps the chap felt that, although engaged in the serious business of enlarging the frontiers of human knowledge, he must cut rather an absurd figure angling around on dry land for anything so elusive as the reptile creation. So Appleby wished him good hunting, and walked on.

There was a further inviting turn, and a further hazel thicket ahead. He was now moving, as it happened, quite silently, since underfoot was a thick mast such as, in a properly organized rural economy, would have been regaling a sizeable herd of swine. The trees from which this neglected fruitage had fallen were a random lot. Beech, oak and chestnut stood shoulder to shoulder – nudging or jostling one another, indeed, in a spirit of robust competition. It wasn't a scene suggesting that at any previous time the Forest of Drool had been the object of much arboricultural care. One had a feeling that in this small patch of England Nature, despite the intrusion of Advanced Herpetology, was still contriving in a more or less primeval fashion.

Appleby rounded the further hazel thicket and at once came upon a changed spectacle. He was looking down into a large and deep basin or natural theatre, such as might have been punched into the yielding globe by some wandering celestial object which had then evaporated in flame long before life on earth began. And an effect of grand combustion, indeed, had for a moment the appearance of strangely lingering on the stage. This was because the glade – for it had to be called that – was ringed with elms in a manner which did perhaps suggest the hand of art, elms being more commonly hedgerow than woodland trees. But the point about these elms was that they were dead, every one. From a few of them tiny shoots were already springing from the bole, so that Nature was perhaps not going to be wholly defeated in the end. But at present the spectacle was as of the aftermath of a forest fire – or better, possibly, of some unfortunate nuclear episode in human history.

The sudden desolation of this scene was very striking, but at the same time a little mitigated by what, near the centre of the basin, had the momentary appearance of a brilliantly sunlit pond. But the pond was too blue to be true, and was in fact a small remaining sea of bluebells. And then Appleby saw that this spectacle had diverted his gaze from something else. There was also a real pond – but one dark and only faintly glinting. Beside it on the grass was seated a strikingly beautiful girl. She was quite immobile, but she was copiously weeping. So fast fell her tears, indeed, that she might have been a garden statue designed softly to replenish the pool below.

II

Appleby's immediate impulse was to withdraw from this strange scene as silently as he had come upon it. His presence had not yet been observed by the dolorous maiden, and his position was such that he could quickly drop out of view. Had the grief of a child been in question, he might have advanced and seen what comfort he could provide. But this was a young adult, not a child, so it would surely be intrusive to march up to her and propose consolation. She had chosen this solitary spot for her weeping, and must be left to get on with it.

Yet Appleby hesitated. He did so, he realized, because of something inherently perplexing in the spectacle before him. It wasn't precisely that there was anything theatrical about it; yet it did hauntingly suggest some familiar deliverance of art. Whether in poetry or in painting – or even, conceivably, in music – he couldn't tell. The ring of dead trees by which the vision was encircled certainly contributed to this effect. So did the girl's attire. There ought to be a rock – Appleby suddenly told himself – of bizarre configuration unknown to geology, and this young person in medieval dress ought to be chained to it. A dragon – preferably rather a comical dragon – ought to be breathing fire in the background. And he himself – a Saint George rather than a Sir John – ought to be advancing to sort things out – on horseback and armed.

This train of thought was interrupted by the girl, who had sprung swiftly and gracefully to her feet. She was tall and slender, and her flowing green gown, which extended to her ankles, was girdled low and seemingly precariously on her hips, with the long embroidered tongue of this sole adornment depending between her knees. The effect was medieval enough, but medieval in a manner mediated through Pre-Raphaelite eyes. The scene upon which Appleby had stumbled might have been a picture telling a story in the manner of Millais or Holman-Hunt and have borne a title like *The Broken Tryst* or *After the Fatal Word*. Only some minor prescriptive element in the hinted fable was missing: perhaps a faded flower, or a love-letter, or even a blood-stained dagger, lying abandoned beside the small dark pool.

Had Sir John Appleby not been indulging this useless fancy he might have more quickly become aware of why the girl had jumped up as she had done. It was because she had registered his presence and was disposed to some positive reaction to it. This, indeed, was so immediately apparent as to make it impossible for him simply to turn round and walk away. The girl's connection with anything to be thought of as a courtly society doubtless extended no further than her dress. Nor could she be described as conducting herself by any means *en princesse*, since her blubbering appearance was of a childish order and she was now looking distinctly cross. Nevertheless Appleby felt that some touch or token of the chivalric was required of him. No dragon showed any sign of turning up; there wasn't even a rude carl or a sorceress disguised as a nun in the offing; nor were the shades of evening beginning alarmingly to fall. Despite all this, however, simply to murmur a civil 'Good afternoon' and then pass on would somehow be inadequate to the small but definite situation that had established itself. So Appleby was about to utter what would, without doubt, have been apt and adequate words when the young woman forestalled him.

'Go away, you horrid beast!' the young woman said loudly. 'I don't want to have anything to do with any of you. And I think my father is very silly to have brought in all that rubbish, and a lot of people like you as well. So there!'

'I beg your pardon – and I shall certainly go away at once. But I think, madam, you must be under some misapprehension. I have not been "brought in" by your father, as you express it, and I think it most improbable that he and I have ever heard of one another.'

'Aren't you one of the people with the wardrobe?'

'My dear young woman, it must be plain to you that my age precludes my being in employment as a furniture remover.' Appleby had refrained from turning away – for the encounter had now developed into an affair of cross-purposes that amused him. 'So here is another misapprehension, it seems to me.'

'I don't mean *that* sort of wardrobe, you stupid man!' The young woman, as she made this extremely rude speech, stamped what appeared to be a sandalled foot soundlessly on the grass. 'And why are you dressed like a gentleman? It's too absurd!'

'Why do I talk like one, for that matter? Say that it's a deception that I've kept up more or less successfully for years. And now, listen. Get it out of your head that I'm somebody down from London with a pantechnicon. I've left my car on the high road to take a walk through this wood. And I find you sitting in the middle of it, crying your eyes out. You're upset, and I'm sorry.'

'It's not the middle of it. It's the other side, you silly.' The dolorous maiden seemed obstinately addicted to nursery compliments. 'Beyond those dead trees there's the park. And after that there's our house, which is called Drool Court. My name's Cherry Chitfield.' The maiden paused on this. 'Worse luck,' she added gloomily.

'I'm Sir John Appleby, and I live at a place called Long Dream not a hundred miles from here.' Appleby was reflecting that the name of Drool Court rang some faint bell in his head. The Chitfields were probably among the innumerable persons of local consequence known to Judith from her earliest years, but whom he himself could never securely fix in his memory. 'If that dress,' he went on, 'comes out of what you call the wardrobe, then I don't think your father deserves to be reproached at all. It must be a good wardrobe. For the dress is an extremely becoming one.'

'That's why I did agree just to try it on.' Miss Chitfield was visibly mollified by this deft turn given to the conversation. 'But then it came over me again. I don't *want* to be a princess saved from an enchanter. And Tibby doesn't want it that way, either.'

'Is Tibby your brother?' Appleby asked innocently.

'Tibby is *not* my brother.' Miss Chitfield stamped her foot again. 'My brother is Mark, and he's quite horrid. Tibby is a friend of mine, and he's to do the rescuing. But we both think it's silly. At least I do, and Tibby agrees with me.' Cherry paused, as if to lend emphasis to this material distinction. 'I want to be a girl just like I am – or almost just like I am – and to be carried off by a sheik.'

'With Tibby as the sheik?'

'Yes, of course. Only my father won't allow it. He insists on the princess thing, with me in this dress, and Tibby wrapped around in a lot of tin, as if he was some sardines. Why can't I have my own way?'

'That's a question, Miss Chitfield, we all frequently ask. But what the answer is in this particular case, I just don't know. Perhaps it is more decorous for a young woman to be rescued from an enchanter by a knight than to be made the lawless prey of a passionate bedouin. Might that be it?'

'I suppose it might. But it doesn't really sound like my father.'

'Then another explanation must be found.' Appleby, who was intolerant even of small obscurities, uttered this with a conviction he was to remember.

'Of course I know that being carried off and ravished by an Arab warrior is frightfully old-hat,' Miss Chitfield went on. 'It happened in Victorian novels by people like

Trollope and Jane Austen. Not that anybody reads *them* now.'

'Some demonstrably do not. However, I agree with you that the theme of the desert lover is a shade *passé*. But just what are we talking about? Is it some species of charades or private theatricals?'

'I think it's a fête, really.' Cherry, who was now perfectly disposed to conversation, had sat down on the grass again. 'I say, you don't happen to be carrying any chocolate, do you? I've missed tea, and I'm getting a bit hungry.'

'I'm afraid not, although I think there are some biscuits in the car. Unfortunately it's rather a long way off.'

'Never mind. I'll just have one of your cigarettes.'

'I'm afraid I'm not provided with cigarettes, either. I do apologize.'

'It doesn't matter.' Cherry had glanced rather suspiciously at Appleby. 'I'm a bit thirsty too, as a matter of fact. But I don't like the look of this pool.'

'Neither do I. You must expect a certain effect of dehydration, Miss Chitfield, after shedding all those tears.'

'Sarky, aren't you?' It was quite amiably that Cherry said this. 'But it's a kind of fête, as I was saying. And with a pageant. Or with some mini-pageants, really.'

'I see. And the brush with the sheik was to be one of them?'

'Yes — and now it's this stupid knight-and-princess thing. But it's a sort of fancy-dress garden party as well. That's why my father has got in all that stuff. Anybody who doesn't want to bother beforehand can hire a costume for an extra five pounds.'

'Dear me! You must move in affluent circles, Miss Chitfield.'

'Yes, we do.'

'And does Tibby?'

'No, he doesn't. That's part of the trouble, I suppose.'

'He can be trusted as a knight, but not as a sheik?'

'I suppose so. It sounds very illogical.'

'It does, indeed. When is this happening?'

'Tomorrow afternoon.'

'And is it a private affair?'

'Of course not.' Miss Chitfield sounded surprised. 'You can buy a ticket in Odger's shop in Linger, and various other places. It's all in aid of a charity, you see. Fallen women or retired governesses or Conservative Party funds – I've forgotten which. We have something of the sort every year – only this time it seems a bigger effort than usual. Mark – that's my brother I told you of – says it's going to be most exquisitely vulgar.'

'I don't see that it need be that, Miss Chitfield. But perhaps it sounds a little on the lavish side.'

'My father has to be lavish, or people would lose confidence in him and we'd all be put in gaol. Or so Mark says.'

'Dear me! Does your father have what may be called a walk in life?'

'He's a financier, if that's what you mean. And a property developer. Mark says property-developing is a dirty word and quite right too.'

'Your brother would appear to be a severe moral-ist.' Appleby, who had dropped companionably down beside Miss Chitfield for a few minutes, got to his feet again. 'I must be on my way,' he said. 'But I leave you my best wishes for the fête. I hope you manage to enjoy it, even if you do have to be a mere medieval princess.'

'I'll *die* first!' Miss Chitfield announced this melo-dramatic fact with considerable passion.

'My dear child' – Appleby was really curious – 'have you made a first-rate family fuss about this piece of nonsense?'

'Yes, I have.'

'But your father is adamant?'

'Yes.' Cherry Chitfield got to her feet too. 'You will come, won't you?' she asked.

'With a ticket from Odger's shop?' The girl's sudden demand had astonished Appleby. 'I'm really afraid –'

'Oh, I can smuggle you in. Not that it looks to me as if a fiver would be beyond you.'

'I suppose it wouldn't – in a good cause.' Appleby was embarrassed by this urgency. 'But, as it happens, tomorrow –'

'I know who you are.'

'I beg your pardon?'

'When you said Long Dream I remembered what Mark had told me about the Applebys there. You're a famous policeman.'

'I've certainly been a policeman in my time. But is it because I'm a policeman –'

'Do come,' Cherry Chitfield said.

Appleby had been a little late for dinner, after all, and was obliged to give an account of himself.

'And you say she was quite grown up?' Judith asked.

'Well, yes – in a sense. Eighteen or nineteen, perhaps. But scarcely what one might call a mature personality.'

'Evidently not. A girl of that age indulging in extravagant grief at being forbidden to indulge in one rather than another very similar bit of play-acting is surely quite absurd? You do seem to have come across somebody uncommonly foolish, John.'

'Well, perhaps so – although I'm not quite convinced of it. But certainly she was a young person not claiming to be flawlessly well bred. I rather felt you'd be likely to know about the Chitfields of Drool Court. But, on consideration, I don't expect you do.'

'Of course I know *of* them. But I just don't happen to *know* them, any more than you do.'

'They're no further off than a good many people we do know. Who would be on visiting terms with them?'

'I suppose the Birch-Blackies are likely to be.' Judith seemed surprised at this inquisition. 'Ambrose has to know everybody, because of the constituency. And Jane is a ceaselessly inquisitive woman.'

'So she is. So these Chitfields aren't immemorial ornaments of that remote part of the county?'

'I've no idea. They certainly weren't at Drool Court when I was a girl. I expect you'd find they'd arrived quite recently. This pageant affair sounds a pushing sort of thing. You make a big noise in aid of some charity or other, and people feel they must look in on it, and pay up, and generally acknowledge your existence. But if this Mr Chitfield simply sent the charity a cheque for the amount he's willing to lay out in mounting his show, then quite probably –'

'Yes, of course. I expect Mark Chitfield – the brother this girl talked about – says much the same thing to his father. He appears to be of a censorious turn of mind, too.'

'I'm not being censorious, John. I'm merely mentioning some unimportant but tedious facts of English social life. But of course I may be quite wrong about those Chitfields.'

'I don't expect so. But, if you are, I'll let you know.'

'You'll let me know!' Lady Appleby stared at her husband. 'You don't mean you propose to *go* to this thing tomorrow?'

'Well, yes – as a matter of fact I do.'

'Then you'd better take Jane Birch-Blackie with you.'

'I think not. My role will be that of a lone hunter.'

'In the appropriate sort of fancy dress?'

'Time is rather short for that. I think I might go as a Commissioner of Metropolitan Police. I have the togs for that in a drawer.'

'But that wouldn't *be* fancy dress, since I suppose you're still entitled to wear those things if you want to.' Judith didn't make this point with any emphasis, since she knew that her husband's suggestion was one there was not the least likelihood of his carrying out. 'Not that it wouldn't be rather fun,' she added. 'You'd scare them all stiff.'

'I'm far from wanting to do that.'

'John, is there anything sensible you *do* want to do about this affair?'

'Well, yes – I believe there is.' Appleby hesitated. 'There was something odd about the way that girl was upset. You might say I'm minded to take a second bite at the Cherry.'

'Very well.' Lady Appleby, if not particularly diverted by this joke, appeared to judge it tactful to acquiesce in any proposal put forward by one so much at a loose end as her superannuated husband appeared to be. 'I have to go shopping in Linger tomorrow morning. I'll get you a ticket from Odger's.'

'And pay for it?'

'Yes, certainly.' Judith rose from the dinner-table. 'And I shan't even ask for my money back,' she added handsomely, 'if all this derring-do proves to be a mare's nest.'

Later that evening, Appleby looked up Richard Chitfield of Drool Court in a work of reference. It was very much a business man's entry, and rather colourless to any reader not hung up on the romance of commerce and industry. Mr Chitfield was the chairman of a group of companies, the activities of which were not particularized, and he was a director of a dozen others. Several City guilds had made him a liveryman, and he was declared to 'control extensive interests' in the Caribbean and the Middle East. He was, in fact, an important man in a far-flung and probably blameless and uninteresting way. Nothing was said about his parentage or education, but as a young man he had married the daughter of Councillor Parker-Perkins, and had apparently kept her on the books ever since. He had a son and two daughters, and his recreations were given as fly-fishing and 'private theatricals'. This last and rather old-fashioned phrase was the only remotely unexpected piece of information intimated. It tied in, no doubt, with what was going to happen at Drool Court next day. All in all, Appleby had no reason to feel that he was going to be very interested in the father of Cherry and Mark Chitfield.

III

Because we speak of the Court of St James's or the Court of Versailles, we are inclined to suppose that when a house is called a 'Court' it must be very grand indeed. But for centuries the word has frequently been tacked on to the proper name of what may be quite a modest manorial dwelling or principal house in a village. And of course if you buy a couple of fields and put up a habitable structure of some sort in the middle of them you are free to call the result 'Windsor Court' or even 'Plantagenet Court' if you have a mind to it.

Drool Court as it now existed was of no great antiquity, although something with the same name had stood on the same ground since the time of the first Elizabeth. Everything now visible was the work of Sir Guy Dawber (an architect of the present century who may be supposed to have eschewed the sister art of painting for an obvious reason) and therefore in the somewhat severe tradition associated with modern country houses in Gloucestershire. There was a great deal of it; when you got inside the principal rooms were lofty and imposing; from without, however, the entire structure had the appearance of being unkindly squashed beneath heavily impending roofs. It was all very solid and English and permanent. If you came upon it unawares during the course of a rural ramble, and took the trouble to find out to whom it belonged, you would be wholly unprompted to hurry to a telephone, call up your stockbroker, and require him to extricate you with all speed from any of the numerous concerns controlled by Mr Chitfield. On the other hand you would not be likely to feel in the presence of anything that charmed the eye or stirred the fancy. And if the occasion of your visit were different, and you were turning up in the expectation of participating in a Watteau-like *fête-champêtre* of easy and light-hearted *divertissement*, it is probable that you would judge the *mise en scène* not particularly appropriate to the mood required.

There were, however, extensive lawns and gardens, with a small park beyond them, and beyond that again the wooded region of Sir John Appleby's first entanglement with the Chitfield fortunes. Had Richard Chitfield been one of the chief noblemen of the country, and generously prompted to entertain everybody who could by any stretch of imagination claim acquaintance with him, these pleasure grounds could have accommodated the whole crowd with no difficulty at all. As it was, and at least at the time of Appleby's fairly prompt arrival, the scene was far from thronged and little in the way of entertainment was as yet going forward.

It was in the character of Robin Hood that Appleby presented himself at the wrought-iron gates of the mansion and handed his ticket to a young woman whom he conjectured to be the elder of the Chitfield daughters. His costume wasn't the consequence of his having reflected, only the day before, that he must frequently have played Robin Hood games as a boy; it represented the first feasible set of garments to have turned up during a rummage of the dressing-up cupboard at Long Dream. The Appleby children having long ago abandoned that sort of entertainment, everything had smelt faintly of the moth balls of a former age, and Appleby was aware of carrying this round with him now. At least the outfit was tolerably complete. There was even a long-bow – which, however, had lost its string, with the result that it couldn't be slung in the prescriptive manner across his shoulder and had to be treated as a walking-stick. This contributed to a faint sense of the ridiculous which he was constrained to own in himself. It was an unaccustomed feeling, and Appleby felt vaguely annoyed by it.

He increasingly misdoubted the whole odd exploit which he had undertaken.

The young woman who took his ticket handed him a programme in return. And she gave him an appraising look as she did so.

'There's going to be a licensed bar open later,' she said.

'Is there, indeed?' This brisk assessment of his predominant interest as likely to be in alcoholic refreshment naturally didn't gratify Appleby very much. 'I suppose outlaws are given to clinking the cannikin whenever the opportunity occurs. If I'd come as a knight, it would be another matter. A true knight is a total abstainer, as Chaucer tells us. "Himself drank water of the well, as did the knight Sir Percivel." So you see –'

'No more of this, for goddes dignitee.' The young woman (thus revealing an academic background) was understandably abrupt. 'You must be the man my sister met in the wood.'

'Yes, Miss Chitfield, I am. My name is John Appleby.'

'I can't think why you've bothered to turn up to all this nonsense. Did Cherry put on one of her turns?'

'I wouldn't describe it as that at all. But she was a little upset. And that brings us back to knights. Is the young man called Tibby still going to be obliged to dress up as one?'

'Oh, yes – I suppose so. He and Cherry had some idiotic affair cooked up, and it would have been perfectly okay and raised the required laugh and tepid applause. But my father just wouldn't have it. I can't think why.'

'Neither can Cherry.' Appleby glanced across the gardens and prepared to proceed, since several people were approaching behind him. 'By the way, when does something begin to happen?'

'Have a look at that programme. Not that it will help you much, since it's all going to be a bit of a muddle. People are supposed to wander around as if it's a garden party. But they're also supposed to watch things in a kind of open-air theatre that has been set up beyond the tennis court. And there's a raffle and a man departing in a hot-air balloon for China or heaven knows where, and an auction sale of pretentious junk, and a band from some regiment or other, and heaven knows what else as well. My father goes in for what you might call overkill. So take your pick, Sir John. Or my lord of Lancaster, perhaps I ought to say.'

'I believe that's a discredited view of Robin Hood's true rank.'

'The English love a lord – so their top bandit has to be one. And Shakespeare, you know, is believed by some to have been a whole committee of lords. And now move on, and let me cope with those tiresome people behind you. How I damn well wish it was bedtime.'

Thus dismissed (not without a touch of the younger Miss Chitfield's uncertain command of the usages of polite society), Appleby did move on. But then Miss Chitfield called after him.

'Oh, I forgot! There's archery down in the meadow. Just your thing, I'd imagine.'

Appleby answered this pleasantry merely by elevating his long-bow in air. He found that he was now manipulating the awkward thing as if it were an alpenstock. And in the distance he had just caught sight of Colonel and Mrs Birch-Blackie. He might have guessed they'd be around, and in his present absurd rig he had no wish whatever to encounter them. He'd minimize the risk of this, he told himself, if he steered clear of that licensed bar.

What had been erected beyond the tennis court was not exactly a theatre, but it was a good deal more than a bare stage or platform. It had an air, indeed, of simplicity and even improvisation, as if it had been run up on the orders of an indulgent parent to meet some passing theatrical ambition on the part of his children. But there was something a little deceptive about this. The whole effect was unobtrusively elegant, and there seemed to be an equally unobtrusive provision of more stage apparatus than would be at all necessary for any casually organized amateur pageant. The frame and setting being provided, that was to say, were themselves professional work of a superior and expensive sort. Richard Chitfield – this was Appleby's conclusion – was the sort of person for whom are designed those advertisements which loudly proclaim themselves as addressed only to persons who will put up with nothing other than the best. Something of this impression had already been conveyed in the conversation of each of his daughters in turn.

There were now a good many people around, and the large paddock which had been appropriated to the purposes of a car park was filling up rapidly. Most of the vehicles were a good deal grander than Judith's little Fiat, which her husband had borrowed for the afternoon. The crush was contrary to Appleby's expectation. Had he been required to give a guess in advance he would have said that this particular manifestation of the charitable concern of Mr Richard Chitfield was bound to be a flop. A fancy-dress ball was one thing, and the English mind had been habituated to the idea for a good many generations. Masque-like entertainments, whether within doors or without, with the spectators taking an intermittent part in whatever action was generated, had gone out of fashion long ago, but could doubtless be promoted and got off the ground for the benefit of persons of antiquarian inclination. But the present rather nebulous entertainment – particularly, perhaps, because so much an affair of broad daylight – was surely something that many people would shy away from.

But it looked as if in these thoughts Appleby was arguing from his own disposition. The participants, or subscribers, or whatever they were to be called, already made a respectable crowd, and were beginning to get on very well together. Many were of course known to one another – and Appleby himself, indeed, was aware of familiar faces. So there was the amusement of failing – or pretending to fail – to recognize acquaintances. Not many people, moreover, appeared to be on their own, and this made Appleby himself feel slightly self-conscious. Acute observers might point him out to one another as a detective hired to mingle with the guests and keep the Chitfield spoons and forks out of their pockets. And what, indeed, was he if not a detective – and one of an officiously self-appointed sort? Or at the least he must be said to have turned up out of vulgar curiosity, since he had to admit that his expectation of deriving simple pleasure from the sundry diversions presently to be on offer was low. It was while thus sunk in gloom, and hard upon rounding a corner of the little theatre, that Appleby came face to face with another Robin Hood.

There was nothing out of the way about this. Why not two Robin Hoods – or half a dozen, for that matter? But this second Robin Hood appeared much struck by the *Doppelgänger* effect: so much so that he halted in his tracks and gave way to audible mirth. There is a species of Englishman who, when motoring on the continent in a car identical with your own, is unable to pass you by without much waving and horn-blowing of an unwarrantably familiar sort. For a moment Appleby thought that here was behaviour of that censurable order. Then he realized that the person with whom he was thus suddenly twinned up was entitled to as much laughter as he cared to indulge in. For Tommy Pride was a family friend. He was also the Chief Constable of the county – or whatever passed itself off as a county in an England of late barbarously chopped up into newfangled regions fondly supposed to conduce to enhanced administrative convenience.

'Good God!' Colonel Pride exclaimed when he had done with laughter. 'Dr Livingstone, I presume?'

Appleby more or less agreed that he was the celebrated explorer, and reflected that Pride's sally, though not strikingly original, was agreeably congruous with the Chief Constable's simple cast of mind. Or rather with his seemingly simple cast of mind, since in point of fact Pride was quite as acute a character as the considerable responsibilities of his office required.

'Taking the day off, Tommy?' Appleby asked.

'Taking the day off, John? Or have they hired you as a private eye?'

'I don't quite know. I was certainly invited to come and look around.'

'By this chap Chitfield?' There was sudden sharp curiosity in Pride's tone.

'I haven't met Chitfield. It was by his younger daughter, as a matter of fact, when I made her acquaintance, quite by chance, yesterday.'

'Well, I'm blessed!' The Chief Constable glanced rapidly round him, apparently to assure himself that this conversation was not being overheard. 'Brought any of the family along with you?'

'No, I haven't. I did suggest it to Judith, but she wouldn't play.'

'No more would Mary. I wanted her to tog up as a Dresden Shepherdess or something, but she turned the idea down.'

'Women are more sensible than men, Tommy.'

'So they are. Utterly irrational, of course. But a damn sight more sensible, as you say. I just thought that if I had Mary with me I'd be less noticeable than on my own.'

'My dear Tommy! Do you mean that you're here as a minion of the law yourself?'

'Not exactly – although I've had to bring a couple of my men. Heaven knows why.'

'Both disguised as Robin Hood?'

'No, no. Distinctions of rank have to be observed – wouldn't you say, John? – even in fancy dress. They're here in their off-duty togs – looking like respectable grocers, no doubt.' Colonel Pride, as he produced these remarks, seemed decidedly unhappy about them. 'Let's take a turn around the show,' he said abruptly. 'Opportunity for a little chat.'

IV

They took a turn around the show, but for some time Colonel Pride was silent. He was certainly in a state of perplexity, and was perhaps hesitating about whether or not to confide in a John Appleby so oddly encountered. It had been with Judith Appleby's family that Pride had been on terms of intimacy in the first place, and although he had taken to the retired Metropolitan Commissioner in a personal way he was a little inclined to think of him as a hardened Londoner, much implicated with tiresome mandarins in the Home Office and elsewhere in Whitehall. Pride believed that the less he was badgered by people of that sort, and the more he was left to make do with county committees and magistrates of his own kidney, the better could he carry out his job of keeping the Queen's peace throughout a substantial tract of rural England. So for the moment he had fallen back upon treating Appleby simply as a fellow-observer of what was at least a sufficiently colourful scene.

When several hundred people have turned up at a kind of garden party, mostly in fancy dress, their behaviour becomes sufficiently unusual to merit the interest of a psychologist. They evince, for one thing, a disinclination to stay put. They become restless or (more learnedly) hyper-kinetic. Perhaps this is the result merely of an impulse to show themselves off in rapid succession to as many people as possible. Or conceivably the act of dressing up as what they are not has symbolized a suppressed impulse to escape from themselves, and they are now dodging around with the obscure intent of carrying this process of release further. Visually, the effect is kaleidoscopic and rather exciting. On the present occasion it was to be supposed that a substantial proportion of the company would be required shortly to settle down as spectators of whatever quasi-dramatic entertainment the open-air theatre was going to offer. A dozen rows of chairs there already awaited them. The kaleidoscopic effect would vanish, and the company take on the appearance of an enormous flower bed. Appleby found himself doubting whether this would be a great success. It was probable, for one thing, that quite a lot of those costumes would be rather uncomfortable when one was required to assume a sedentary position in them for long.

Colonel Pride's mind appeared to be moving like Appleby's, since when he did speak it was to take up this more or less superficial aspect of the occasion.

'All this toggery is straight theatrical stuff, wouldn't you say? Designed for the stage, I mean, and to be seen at a distance and under artificial light.'

'Not quite all of it. There are women in their grandmothers' riding-habits and men in their grandfathers' uniforms.'

'Perfectly true. You show you're among the nobs that way, eh? Tell a lot about a fellow from what he chooses to masquerade as. Look at that pirate over there. Timid little chap, I expect, always feeling he's been done down and robbed by somebody. He'd have come as a highwayman if he could sit a horse.'

'Very probably. And I wonder whether appropriate mounts are barred? I'd rather fancy turning up as a rajah on my private elephant. Or as a sheik on a camel.' Appleby glanced swiftly at Pride. 'Incidentally, there's a young man, a friend of the Chitfields, who wants to come as a sheik, but isn't being let.'

'It sounds rather arbitrary, that. Hard to see any offence in it. I could understand this fellow Chitfield not much caring for a chap turning up as Jesus Christ, armed with a scourge with which to whip the money-changers out of the temple.' Making this very profane joke, Pride chuckled innocently. 'A top money-changer in his way, I take this Richard Chitfield Esquire to be.'

'A usurer, you mean?'

'No, no – just the ordinary City scum. Entirely respectable until somebody obliges us to turn up on him with a warrant.'

'I see.' Appleby wasn't sure that he saw much – or not on the score of this stiffly intolerant speech. But it did seem to him that Pride had been quite uninterested in his oblique reference to the entertainment proposed by Cherry Chitfield and the young man called Tibby. The small mystery attached to this (which Appleby had so perplexedly to acknowledge to himself as the sole reason of his being now at Drool Court) was no part of Pride's own pigeon. Just what Pride's pigeon was, and why a couple of his men in plain clothes were on the spot as it were to pluck the bird, it was high time to find out. If Tommy Pride, that was to say, was prepared to play.

'Tommy,' he said firmly, 'just what is this nonsense about your having a couple of plain-clothes men uselessly lost in that mob? I can understand those Chitfields wanting a spot of security, modern times being as they are. But I'd expect them to do their hiring from a private firm.'

'Quite right, if all that they apprehended was a bit of pilfering, and so on. Bobbies much too thin on the ground, these days, to be deployed on that sort of thing, even on a cash-down basis. If there's a threat of public disorder it's another matter. We have to be there, although we may send in a bill to the concern that has generated the risk of trouble. But that's all beside the point here. My men are on the spot simply on the orders of my boss in London.'

'Come off it, Tommy. You haven't got a boss in London.'

'True enough, in a fashion. But it's complicated in various ways, as you very well know. For example, there are things I'm authorized to do only if I ask the Home Secretary to instruct me to do them. But more often, of course, it's just a matter of receiving a word in the ear that this or that spot of cooperation would be helpful. It's going to be helpful to have these men here this afternoon. God knows why. But I've said that before.'

'So you have.' It was Appleby's turn to look cautiously round, and he saw that for the moment he and the Chief Constable had achieved complete seclusion. 'Your men aren't here at any suggestion emanating from Richard Chitfield?'

'Not so far as I know. But I don't know much. That's my point, isn't it?'

'Seemingly so. Just what are your men meant to *do*?'

'Keep an eye open.' Colonel Pride was suddenly breathing rather heavily. 'Believe me, John, those were the very words.'

'I see.' This time Appleby did see. 'Your men are here so that – following some incident not communicated to you – their having been here can be pointed to by some wretched Minister as showing that all proper precautions had been taken?'

'It may be no more than that. Arranging a presence, as they say – but denying me the information that could make it an effective presence. I can imagine one of those bloody leather-bottoms in Whitehall thinking up that one.'

'One wonders why he should want to think it up.'

'Quite so, John. And I'm here myself to try to find out. That's a muddled notion, perhaps. But it's the best I can manage.'

'Has it occurred to you that this entire fête may be a cover for something else?'

'Yes, it has. But I don't think it is. Or not quite. I suspect it was all arranged as a piece of routine charitable endeavour by these damned Chitfields, and that then somebody has seen the chance of exploiting it to a differ- ent end. And I'm going to be gestured at if something goes wrong. "We alerted poor old Pride," they'll say, "and he did his best."'

'In fact, you're standing by to carry the can?'

'Well, to be fair, John, those button-headed desk-hoppers don't see it quite that way. But the whole thing makes sense only in terms of some discreditable diplomatic equivocation. You know the kind of thing. Letting something happen because you don't particularly see why it needn't be let happen. But having some face-saving gesture to make. Not in public, of course. As part of a smooth confidential reply to an indignant *aide-mémoire*, or whatever they call it.'

'Deep waters, Tommy. What about some sort of hush-hush conference or rendezvous going on here – one that other interested parties have been conceivably tipped off about with the chance of awkward and even violent consequences?'

'Nothing more likely. Nothing more absurd and bizarre, and therefore nothing more likely. As the next thing to a kid in Military Intelligence during the war, you know, I brushed up against such lunacies often enough. They were incubated by crackpot dons recruited for the purpose and hatched in houses not unlike Drool Court.'

'And very successfully at times.'

'Well, that's true.' Pride, a fair-minded man, nodded gloomily. 'And I have to admit I may be taking too dark a view of the thing. There is a suggestion that some sort of genuine action may be called for. Down there in the car park I have a fellow in uniform waiting for further instructions, if any, on the VHF. Not that they say "instructions", you know. They say "briefing", because they feel it's more polite.'

'Contingency planning,' Appleby said. 'There's a mania for it.'

'Just that. If we're told in advance just what *may* happen, we may go gossiping round when it *doesn't* happen – and sombody in some embassy or other is going to be offended. So the blasted contingency is kept like a cat in a bag till the last moment. And now, my dear John, let's join the crush again, and keep that confounded eye on things.'

But quite soon Appleby and Colonel Pride parted company. Two Robin Hoods walking shoulder to shoulder perhaps rather uncomfortably suggested to them the spectacle of a couple of police constables prudently twinned up in a particularly rowdy district. Not that Appleby – however it might be with his companion – had any wish to veil his true identity. His garments were a concession to the occasion, and not a disguise. He had been drawn to the fête by the sense of a small mystery. And now, if Pride was right, it seemed probable that it was harbouring a larger one as well. Even so, no retired top policeman could have dreamed of anything so indecorous as turning up at it in a feigned character. Appleby had declared himself to the elder Miss Chitfield; he now looked around for the younger – who, he hoped, might be come upon in the company of her young man. Tibby, it occurred to him, was really a girl's name: a diminutive of Isabel which Professor McIlwraith would probably declare to be imported from Scotland. Perhaps in this case it was short for Theobald. In neither form, somehow, did it sound a very promising name for a sheik.

Professor McIlwraith himself, as it happened, was the next acquaintance Appleby encountered. His presence seemed a little surprising, since one would somehow not have expected a severe scholar to turn up at such an affair. He was, of course, still virtually a stranger to Appleby, and it was conceivable that he put in much of his retirement roving the countryside in quest of just such diversions as Mr Chitfield was affording today. But he had not accommodated himself to the spirit of the occasion by assuming fancy dress, and he was thus among the small minority of those present who might be described as rationally attired. Perhaps, however, he had come as an Eminent Lexicographer (just as Appleby might have come as a Commissioner of Police). Before he opened his mouth you could almost guess that he was that. Like the man in Yeats's poem, Appleby thought, he seemed to cough in ink.

'Good afternoon, Sir John,' McIlwraith said genially. 'Worse than death, would you be inclined to say?'

'I beg your pardon?'

'One sometimes speaks of a fate as that, does one not?'

'Oh, I see.'

'The jest is a little blunted, I fear, because the two words are only approximately homonymic. And doubtless there are worse fêtes than this one – although one is conscious of it as being on the disorganized side. It is an unexpected pleasure to find you at it.' Professor McIlwraith accompanied this polite remark with a sharp glance.

'I may be said to have turned up a little on impulse.'

'It is almost so with me. But the son of the house, as it happens, was one of my last pupils.'

'Mark Chitfield?'

'The same. It was, of course, as a postgraduate student, as I had long since ceased to have any concern with undergraduates. He is a clever young man, and came to me professing to have discovered an interest in phonemic analysis. Has phonemic analysis, by any chance, been among your own studies, Sir John?'

'No, I can't say that it has.' Appleby felt this to be a shade bald. 'Not hitherto,' he added – rather as if at this very moment the interest in question was rising up in him.

'Ah! Well, I fear that in Mark Chitfield's case "professing" was what is vulgarly termed the operative word. He wanted to remain in residence at the university to pursue what I conjecture to have been less intellectual interests, and phonemic analysis was the first resource to come into his head.'

'It is something that he had heard of it, I suppose.'

'Perfectly true. It is to be accounted to him for virtue, no doubt. And I rather took to young Mark. We have maintained our acquaintance – and hence my turning up here this afternoon.'

'I'd rather like to meet Mark.'

'My dear Sir John, you are about to do so.' McIlwraith was glancing over Appleby's shoulder. 'For here he is.'

Appleby turned round, and found himself confronting a spectacle of the most horrendous and revolting sort. The crippled creature bent nearly double before him was dressed mainly in dirt and rags – and more, seemingly, in the former than the latter. At a casual glance he appeared to have only one tooth, one ear, and an eye that had been knocked sideways in his head. It was a head, however, that wore a battered crown; his rotting clothes were here and there slashed and patched with silk and ermine; two burdensome leather bags chained to his waist were dragging behind him; at his side hung a broken sword.

'Good afternoon,' this appearance said urbanely, and without waiting for Professor McIlwraith to speak. 'May I introduce myself? I am one of the Seven Deadly Sins. Just which, I haven't yet determined. It must attend upon the event. Lust attracts me, I am bound to say. But I also have a fancy for Ire.'

'This is Mark Chitfield,' McIlwraith said with surprising composure – and even, it seemed, with approval. 'Mark, this is Sir John Appleby, a neighbour of mine.'

'How do you do?' Mark put out a hand that was disconcertingly clean and well tended. 'These assumed identities do give scope to the confessional impulse, wouldn't you say? I suggested to my father that he might appropriately appear as Avarice, in which case I'd myself plump for Sloth. Have you brought Maid Marian with you, sir?'

'I'm afraid not.' Appleby gave Cherry Chitfield's brother an appraising look. 'I suspect,' he said, 'that your garb at least makes a nice change.'

'Just that.' Mark's begrimed face brightened unexpectedly with a not unattractive grin. 'Most of them got

41

up a bit above themselves, wouldn't you say? Walked into Drool straight out of *le grand siècle* or *la belle époque*. My own idea has been to afford a juster representation of the human condition.'

'Quite so,' Appleby said. The attraction of this young man for Professor McIlwraith, he supposed, consisted in his command of a certain linguistic sophistication. As to whether Mark was at all likeable, he reserved his judgement. Cherry had called her brother 'horrid', but by this she might have meant only that he was too clever for her. Perhaps the elder Miss Chitfield was more his match. She had certainly given tokens of having enjoyed the same blessings of higher education. What all three children had in common was a tendency to evince a disenchanted view of things.

'But you've taken a different line yourself,' Mark said to Appleby on a concessive note. 'Robbing the rich and giving to the poor, and all that. Incidentally, there's another chap around in Lincoln green. I caught a glimpse of him a few minutes ago. Is he your second-in-command, sir? He doesn't look exactly like Friar Tuck.'

'He's Colonel Pride,' Appleby said. 'And your Chief Constable.'

'Good Lord! You lot do seem to be keeping tabs on us. We're a shady crowd, you see.' Mark had offered this last remark to McIlwraith, who had appeared to be a good deal startled to learn that top policemen were so thick on the ground. 'And I've warned my father often enough. It must all catch up with him one day.'

'I'm here simply because your sister Cherry invited me.' Appleby had thought poorly of Mark's last joke. 'And I've been looking out for her.'

'I'm looking out for her myself, as a matter of fact. I'm afraid she's up to some mischief. Along with that juvenile admirer of hers.'

'The young man called Tibby?'

'That's right — Tibby Fancroft. Has Cherry been chattering about him?'

'His name cropped up during our short conversation yesterday.'

'Cherry imagines our parents have a down on Tibby – simply because he isn't an infant stockbroker. It's quite untrue. My father's rather soft on Tibby, really. He probably thinks the child is just about right for his younger daughter, and that Tibby could be fixed up in some harmless niche easily enough. I forget whether you've met our Tibby, Prof?'

'I have not had that pleasure, so far.' McIllwraith seemed unoffended by this facetiously familiar mode of address.

'Tibby's also lying low at the moment. My father won't be at all pleased if they fly in the face of parental command.'

'In the matter of the rescued or ravished maiden?' Appleby asked.

'Just that. Cherry seems to have been uncommonly communicative.'

'It was much on her mind. Does your father go in for taking a stern line with his children, Mr Chitfield?'

'Not in the least. He didn't even disapprove of phonemic analysis – about which the Prof has no doubt told you. It's just that about this particular thing he appears to have a bee in his bonnet. It puzzles me, as a matter of fact. And now I think I'll take a look at the archery. It was a fashionable sport with the gentry until superseded by lawn tennis about a hundred years ago.'

'It is a curious fact,' Professor McIllwraith said, 'that lawn tennis was originally introduced into these islands under the name of "sphairistike". As you will recall, Sir John, *sphairistikos* was the classical Greek term for any sort of ball-game. Its adoption affords a striking instance of the continued vitality of that ancient tongue as an instrument of education in the latter part of the nineteenth century.'

'"Striking" is just the word,' Mark said, 'although "pit-pat" might have been more accurate. As for archery,

43

the gentlemen liked it, since it constrained the ladies to exhibit what was called their figures – and before the invention of the *brassière*, I imagine. But it was a long time before even lawn tennis permitted them to exhibit their legs.'

'It is a remarkable circumstance,' McIlwraith said, 'that, in French, *brassières* were originally leading-strings for infants.'

'I must look round for my friends the Birch-Blackies,' Appleby said disingenuously.

'I'll come a bit of the way with you,' Mark said promptly. 'We'll see you later, Prof.' And with this he led Appleby away without ceremony. 'As a matter of fact,' he then went on, 'I'm going to slip into the house and get rid of these togs. The joke's rather boring.'

'Well, yes – enough is enough.'

'And that's true of the Prof as well, wouldn't you say? In your time, I believe, one talked about a sleeping dictionary as a nice means of picking up a foreign language. The Prof might be called a peripatetic one, it seems to me. And nobody would want to go to bed with him.'

'Demonstrably not.'

'You ought to have a go at the archery yourself. You and the Chief Constable can compete at hitting the gold. I believe that's the expression.'

'I believe it is.'

It was with no great reluctance that Appleby parted from young Mark Chitfield a couple of minutes later. He was a clever young man, and his determined flippancy was not to be accounted seriously against him. But for the time being, Appleby felt, enough was enough, not only of the eminent retired lexicographer but of his late abortive pupil as well.

V

Appleby made his own way to the archery field a little later, having discovered that nothing was going to happen in the theatre for some time. It was during this walk that he saw his first sheik. Sheiks were in those days very thick on the ground – or were so if the word be taken to mean any adequately prosperous person self-evidently from the Middle East. Appleby saw a score of such visitors whenever he went to London, which it was apparent they thought of as an emporium rather than a city of historic interest. Being thus commanded by a laudable and single-minded impulse to spend money, they didn't often stray beyond the capital. But here was at least a fancy-dress sheik attending the fête at Drool Court.

Appleby, rather oddly, had got all this way in his thinking before Tibby Fancroft returned to his head. When this did happen he concluded that the figure he had just glimpsed in a crowd must be Tibby, defiantly attired in his forbidden costume. Then he realized that this was not necessarily so. Because of the very abundance of authentic sheiks on the metropolitan scene – not to speak of television – it was likely that dressing up in such a character might come into anybody's head. This mightn't be Tibby at all. Tibby might be quite elsewhere in the crush, blamelessly attired as a medieval knight. And there was yet a further possibility. The man mightn't be pretending to be a real sheik. He might be pretending to be Lawrence of Arabia pretending to be a real sheik. And here a kind of infinite regress became theoretically possible. Appleby had glimpsed a real sheik who, for some deep purpose of his own, was pretending to be Lawrence of Arabia pretending to be a real sheik. Come to think of it, an aristocratic Arab of a satirical turn of mind might hit upon this little joke readily enough.

And now Appleby saw his second sheik. The first had been a specimen of the portly kind, vaguely suggesting a sack of flour mysteriously endowed with a power of waddling locomotion. This one was of the tall, spare and stately sort, whose progress was as smooth as that of some proud galleon moving over a calm sea. He was featured like a hawk, a fact scarcely obscured by the large dark glasses through which he surveyed the vulgar herd around him. Could *this* be Tibby? If it was, then Tibby was wasting his time and talent upon any theatricals of a merely amateur order. There were possibly half a dozen men, not more, on the London stage who could put on this commanding turn.

The second sheik, like the first, disappeared in the crowd, and Appleby found himself looking around for a third. He had a brief vision of an *embarras* of sheikdom fortuitously irruptive upon Mr Chitfield's party; even of rival business men from the neighbourhood of Lombard Street or Cheapside, thus disguised and indignantly confronting one another, like two ladies who have chanced to buy the same clever little frock from the same clever little woman in Hampstead.

But for the moment nothing disconcerting of this order happened, and Appleby was able to take a look at the archery. Some of those taking part in it were congruously dressed, so that they might have been limbering up for an engagement at Senlac Hill or Agincourt. Others were less in any such established picture, since they were drawing their bows with difficulty while habited as Teddy bears, golliwogs, Daleks, witches and deep-sea divers. Nevertheless the contests were being more or less expertly conducted, and it was to be conjectured that some local archery club had consented to turn up to lend colour to the occasion. Gentlemen were instructing ladies in the command of this former glory of England's yeomen at arms. Some of them were doing so in the spirit touched upon by Mark Chitfield when reflecting on the charms of the female form. There is a certain hazard to life in archery when conducted in too lighthearted and casual a fashion, since a long-bow is quite as lethal a weapon as a revolver. But the present exercises appeared to be prudently regulated in that regard. Appleby watched the proceedings until he remembered that he was carrying a bow himself – whereupon he was prompted to withdraw. A bow without a bow-string is a useless affair. He felt that he would in a sense be letting down the side if suddenly summoned by an officious marshal to the mark.

Walking back towards the house, he wondered about its owner. Where was Mr Richard Chitfield? Where, for that matter, was Mrs Chitfield, née Parker-Perkins? Having thrown open their grounds and clearly put up a good deal of money in the interest of this charitable effort, they might have been expected to be moving around in a modestly welcoming way that would distinguish them from their guests. But Appleby could see nobody exhibiting that kind of comportment, whether in everyday clothing or in fancy dress. Then he remembered that Mr Chitfield's leisure, when not given over to fly-fishing, was devoted to private theatricals. The forthcoming pageant in the open-air theatre was probably his particular concern, and he might well be there now, supervising the final arrangements. Having some curiosity about Cherry's heavy father, Appleby moved in that direction again.

The lawns in front of the mansion were crowded – so crowded that any individual was liable to vanish from view seconds after one sighted him. Prudent persons were already entering a large marquee in the hope, if not of champagne, at least of strawberries and cream. There was a prematurely expectant crowd round the hot-air balloon: at present a floppy pear-shaped affair in a variety of brilliant colours, the preliminary inflating of which was being supervised by a man attired – uncomfortably and surely needlessly – as if his destination was going to be the moon. His actual project, whatever it was, appeared to be mixed up with an obscure competition involving the setting adrift of less ambitious gas-filled balloons of the children's party sort. The military band, perched at the end of a terrace, laboured valiantly at its instruments without much hope of arresting either an ear or an eye.

At a short distance beyond the large marquee there were two smaller ones, and these at present were unfrequented. Or so Appleby thought until, as he was about to pass them by, a figure emerged from between them. It was the figure of a man. Indeed, it was Appleby's third sheik.

This sheik, unlike the earlier sheiks, didn't at once disappear again from view. In fact he approached Appleby in a wholly affable manner, and then paused to address him with confidence.

'If it's the bar you're looking for,' he said, 'these are n-b-g, old boy.' He paused as if to assure himself that his hearer was one to whom this demotic expression was intelligible. 'They're only the damned toilets.'

'The bar should no doubt be one's earlier port of call.' Appleby saw that this sheik also wore dark glasses, but wasn't otherwise made up so as to pass for any sort of authentic Arab. 'I'm afraid I haven't seen it myself.'

'It mayn't be open yet, come to think of it,' the third sheik said unhappily. 'They probably have to keep pub hours.'

'I don't think so.' Appleby was glad to have an encouraging consideration to advance to this wanderer in a thirsty desert. 'I believe one gets a special sort of licence for an affair like this, and can keep open all the time.'

'Well, I'll just take a walk round and see,' the third sheik said, brightening a little. 'The name is Pring,' he added, as if recalling a necessary courtesy.

'How do you do, Mr Pring? My name is Appleby. I

hope you won't feel awkward when you do find the bar. Arabs, you know, are not supposed to drink alcohol.'

'That's right!' Mr Pring seemed both impressed and depressed by this consideration. 'Something to do with their religion, it must be. And I wouldn't like not to show respect, Mr Appleby.'

'I don't think there's any danger of that.' Appleby was favourably struck by this honourable if confused feeling on Mr Pring's part. 'By the way, have you noticed that several other people have come in Arab costume?'

'Is that so? I haven't seen them. And it's not what you might call very original, is it? I'd have thought of something better, I think I may say, if it hadn't been for Mr Chitfield.'

'You discussed the matter with Mr Chitfield?' Although not hitherto really very interested in the parched Mr Pring, Appleby was suddenly alert.

'Chitfield asked me to come and support his fête. And, business associations being as they are, Mr Appleby, it seemed to me I oughtn't to refuse. Chitfield and me, that's to say, having been partners in this and that.' Mr Pring paused, and perhaps felt that this suggested an implausible degree of commercial elevation. 'Not, mark you, that I put myself in Richard Chitfield's bracket – not by a long way. Chitfield is one of the biggest men we have. But I'm substantial, Mr Appleby, I can fairly say. It's twelve years now since Mrs Pring and I had our first executive-type home, and we haven't stood still since then by no means.'

'I am delighted to hear it. Is Mrs Pring with you today – as an Arab lady, perhaps?'

'Mrs Pring, sir, is here as Joan of Arc. It was entirely her own idea, that was, and I'm bound to say she looks uncommonly well.'

'I don't doubt it, and I hope I may have the pleasure of meeting her. So you consulted Mr Chitfield and asked him whether he thought it would be a good idea if you turned up as a sheik or emir or person of that sort?'

'Well, no, Mr Appleby. That wasn't the way of it at all.

Chitfield brought the idea forward, and was really quite pressing about it.'

'I see. Do you happen to know whether he made similar specific suggestions to any other of his – um – colleagues and associates?'

'I couldn't say, I'm sure.' Mr Pring was a little surprised by this question. 'He's often very fertile with his suggestions, Chitfield is. But in the business way, I mean. Throws out this and that, like he was Napoleon giving tips to his generals.'

'He sounds most impressive. A dominating character, no doubt. Would you say that he was fond of his joke, Mr Pring?'

'He can tell the right sort of story in the right place, Chitfield can. Never before the ladies, you know, and not even to a barmaid. It's a touchstone, that, Mr Appleby, I think you'll agree. Never a dirty word to the girl drawing the beer, and you can tell yourself you're a perfect gentleman.'

'It's something we ought all to remember, Mr Pring. So Mr Chitfield likes a laugh in the right place. Would you say he was any sort of practical joker? It's not quite the same thing.'

'Definitely not.' Mr Pring was again surprised. 'He just wouldn't give time to such a notion. Always plenty on his plate. A true man of affairs is Richard Chitfield.'

VI

But were they, Appleby asked himself as he walked away, conceivably shady affairs? Tommy Pride had referred to Richard Chitfield as 'just the ordinary City scum', but that had been a matter of the routine and more or less harmless intolerance of a man contemptuous of all money-making other than that of earning an honest day's pay. Nothing whatever could be founded on it. Mark Chitfield made a joke – also with a touch of routine to it – to the effect that one day the entire Chitfield family was bound to end up in gaol. Of such a freakish pleasantry there was nothing to be made either. Cherry's quarrel with her father might be so much petulant nonsense, blown up out of some passing irritation on his part. Chitfield's telling his humble associate Pring to dress up as an Arab might hitch on to this in some obscure and trivial way. What really needed chewing over was the extraordinary circumstance of Pride's having been asked (and with what looked like typical Secret Service hush-hush flummery) to place this overblown garden fête under surveillance – something he had in fact done in a singularly sparing way. But the fête was Chitfield's creation. It was Chitfield who deserved a long straight look-over. Appleby decided he was hunting for the elusive host of the afternoon.

So he moved on to the theatre, and presently found that a good many people were doing the same thing. It occurred to him to glance a little more attentively than he had done so far at the programme which the elder Miss Chitfield had given him on his arrival. It seemed that the theatrical part of the entertainment was due to start in ten minutes – which probably meant that it would start in half an hour. It didn't sound too promising in terms of powerful dramatic experience. Various local groups, societies and coteries, it seemed, had undertaken to present a series of scenes or sketches linked together on the grand theme of English History. There were to be some Ancient Britons hunting bears and other equally Ancient Britons putting up a tough fight against Julius Caesar and his legions. There was to be (what ought to interest Appleby) a scene of outlawry in Sherwood Forest, with appropriate speeches from *As You Like It* thrown in. Several troops of Boy Scouts were combining to enact the relief of Mafeking, in which the part of Colonel R. S. S. Baden-Powell was to be sustained by Master William Birch-Blackie. And there was to be much else. It would all be great fun, clearly, for the senior Birch-Blackies and such other spectators as had loved ones cavorting on the stage. On others it might a little pall.

And not everybody was making for the theatre. Appleby was amused to see several men actually moving with a certain unobtrusiveness against the stream. And some of these recalcitrant persons appeared to be among the more exuberant of Mr Chitfield's guests, at least if they were to be judged by their attire. As Mark Chitfield had observed, the majority of fancy costumes on view betrayed a certain yearning after exalted station, or at least an enhanced social consequence, on the part of their wearers: hence all the gentlemen in powder and knee-breeches and ladies in eighteenth-century *grande tenue*. Any note of the broadly comical or grotesque (as with Mark's own Deadly Sin) was confined to a scattering of males, and it was among these that the prospect of the theatrical entertainment didn't seem to be much fun. One of the deep-sea divers, a couple of fantastically painted circus clowns, a Chinaman, a man in an ass's head presumably to be thought of as Shakespeare's transmogrified Bottom were among the defectors to be remarked.

Perhaps like Mr Pring, these more enterprising persons were sloping off in quest of the bar.

It was while Appleby was taking note of this that Mark appeared again, and this time he was accompanied by the hitherto absent Cherry. The young man had carried out his intention of changing into what might be called mufti; it was mufti of considerable elegance; he had moreover found time for a drastic scrub-up as well. These changes had turned him very definitely into the son of the house, in which role he was carrying out those duties of an amiable host to be expected of his still invisible father. The effect however was not without a hint of indulgence or even disdain for all the childishness round about him which those who detected it couldn't have been too pleased with. Appleby didn't make much of his sister's attire. Cherry was wearing a sola topi and a trouser-suit of white drill which may have been designed to establish her either as a tropical explorer or as a memsahib tagging along behind a tiger hunt. She would have looked quite well on the elephant upon which Appleby had earlier fancied himself in the character of a rajah. She was certainly remote from being any sort of medieval princess.

'Hullo, Sir John!' she said. 'Patty told me you'd turned up. Good on you!'

'It's all being most enjoyable, Miss Chitfield.' And Appleby added – perhaps as judging this response to be on the conventional side – 'Has Patty gone to bed?'

'Why ever should she do that? Is she feeling ill?'

'No – but she said she was longing for bedtime.'

'Our parents oughtn't to have named her Patience,' Mark said. 'It's a shockingly rustic name, for one thing. And, for another, it was tempting providence. Patty has turned out to be without an atom of the quality in her composition. Not like me. I'm cascading it over this whole idiotic revel.'

'No doubt you're doing your best,' Appleby said. 'I

53

hope, by the way, that one of you is going to introduce me to your parents. I'd like to pay them my respects.'

'It would have to be right-about-turn for my mother.' Mark jerked a thumb over his shoulder. 'She'll be in that enormous tent, presiding over the people who are dishing out the refreshments.'

'She's a sensible woman at times,' Cherry said concessively, 'and can put first things first. But my father is bound to be in the theatre, so come along. It's very much his thing.'

'So I supposed. I've just met, incidentally, one of his business associates. At least he claimed to be that. A drouthy character called Pring.'

'Good Lord!' Mark said. 'Is Pring out already? It must be the work of the Parole Board. They've been suborned.'

This was presumably Mark Chitfield's percurrent bad joke. His sister ignored it, and took Appleby rather engagingly by the arm.

'I suppose they'll be beginning with the Ancient Britons,' she said. 'All skin-tights and woad. When it gets to Sherwood, Sir John, you'll be able to join in. Daddy is very hot on audience participation. Perhaps we'll have quite a lot of it.'

Cherry Chitfield was far from being the woebegone maiden of the day before. She was in good spirits. In fact she was distinctly excited. Appleby took another glance at her attire, and found himself wondering about Tibby Fancroft, that other elusive character on the fringes of the scene. He had formed a hypothetical picture of Tibby as not among the most dominant of males, and he suspected that whatever Tibby was doing at that moment it was something Cherry had put him up to. But this was guesswork such as competent policemen never indulge in. Appleby told himself that he wasn't at Drool Court as a competent policeman. Tommy Pride was that. He himself had come along simply as an elderly gentleman with time on his hands. But this didn't mean that he wasn't to ask questions when they came into his head.

'A fête on this scale,' he said to Mark, 'and one with such a variety of goings-on, must take a good deal of trouble to mount. And, of course, a good deal of time as well. I suppose it's all planned well in advance?'

'Very definitely. My father has been devoting much of his hard-won leisure to it over the past six months. Or when he isn't catching fish. Not that we're sure he does *catch* fish. He probably employs somebody to do just that. It's called delegating responsibility.'

'He believes in getting everything cut and dried?' Appleby was not to be diverted by this rather tired joke on Mark's part.

'Oh, yes. It all goes down on paper at the start, and everybody has to stick to it.'

'The fancy-dress element in this present affair, for instance: it wouldn't have been a recent afterthought?'

'Distinctly not. I think we began to hear about it before Christmas. Wouldn't that be right, Cherry?'

'Yes – and then off and on ever since. It's all rather boring, really – organizing like mad for a stupid party. Let's put Sir John in the front row, Mark, and then see if we can find Daddy. He'll be hearing somebody their lines at the eleventh hour, or gumming on their whiskers.'

It was with reluctance that Appleby thus found himself dumped in a position of some prominence and then left to his own devices. The auditorium, which lay in bright sunshine, was filling up. In front of it, and before the stage, a curtain hung incongruously against the sky, supported on cables slung between two beech trees. There was a buzz of talk and a smell of trodden grass. Within further curtained-off areas it was clear that numerous preparatory activities were going on, although it was improbable that they could conceal whole hordes of Ancient Britons and centuries of Romans.

'Excuse me,' a woman's voice said behind Appleby's ear, 'but can you tell me what a romantic rescue is?'

'A romantic rescue? I'm afraid I don't understand you,

madam.' Appleby had turned round, and saw a middle-aged woman poring over her programme.

'That's what it says. "A Romantic Rescue". Do you think it might mean Robert Browning and Elizabeth Barrett? I'd have thought that a little too literary – wouldn't you? For this sort of audience, I mean.'

'Possibly so.'

'And not really a very central incident in English History.'

'Certainly not that.' This gratuitously talkative person, Appleby thought, was of somewhat captious disposition. 'But it's clear that they've strung a very miscellaneous collection of turns together, isn't it? People must have come along offering to put on this and that, and they've just imposed some vague pattern on the result. How fortunate that it is so fine an afternoon.'

Thus bringing this conversation to a decorous close, Appleby squared himself on his chair again and turned to his own reflections. It seemed to him that 'A Romantic Rescue', although probably meant to refer to the medieval Cherry preserved from an enchanter by her knight, might by a little stretch of meaning cover the modern Cherry carried off by her desert lover. Perhaps the title had been arrived at in a spirit of compromise when the admissibility of Cherry's own wishes in the matter had still been in debate within her family.

'I thought you might know because I saw you with the young Chitfields.' Appleby had not, after all, shaken off the woman behind him. 'How delightful they are.'

'Yes, indeed.'

'Or my husband might know, since he is intimate with Richard Chitfield, and Richard is so much the moving spirit in this sort of thing. I wonder whether you know my husband?'

'I don't think I have that pleasure, madam.' Appleby had been obliged to turn round again. His interlocutor wore a pair of wings – obviously wings of the most expensive sort – and a dress seemingly designed to suggest the firmament on a starry night. She also carried a wand with a further twinkling star at the end of it. She might have been the Good Fairy in a pantomime, but was probably intended to be of a superior order to that. A Fairy Queen, in fact – and not Spenser's but Shakespeare's. Here, in other words, was Titania – or this was an assumption so substantial that Appleby judged it possible to proceed on it. 'Is it your husband,' he asked, 'who is sustaining the part of Bottom?'

'Yes, it is.' Titania was delighted by this feat of ratiocination. 'Rupert has very considerable textile interests in the Far East. So I thought nothing could be more appropriate for him than Nick Bottom the weaver. I had the ass's head specially made for him so that he has no need to take it off. He can't eat or drink, of course. But it has a cunning little window set inside the mouth.'

'Most ingenious. I congratulate you.' Appleby reflected that poor Bottom couldn't have been making for the bar, after all. 'And have you brought along a friend,' he asked, 'in the character of Oberon?'

'Well, no. But how delightful that you are a lover of Shakespeare! Rupert is a great lover of Shakespeare. You really must meet him.'

'I shall hope for an opportunity.' Appleby, a hardened proponent of what used to be called the forms, produced this response unflinchingly. He didn't know this confounded woman from Adam's Eve, but it was necessary to be civil to her.

'Of course I know who you are, Sir John. Ambrose Birch-Blackie pointed you out to me earlier in the afternoon. He had just spotted you, and was hoping to have a chat with you later. I am Cynthia Plenderleith.'

'How do you do? I think the curtain is about to go up.'

'I don't think so. They are merely testing it. I do hope Rupert will be back by the time the pageant really begins. He had to slip away, he said. I can't think why.'

Appleby might have said, 'I suppose he wants a bit of hush.' Or even, 'Perhaps he's looking for the loo.' But as neither of these conjectures was admissible in polite conversation with a Queen of the Fairies he held his peace.

'He said he might be away for half an hour. So meanwhile, Sir John, I feel quite unattended.'

'I'm sure you need never, in fact, be that.' Appleby produced this slightly laboured compliment while wondering whether it was requisite that he should move back a row and himself squire the lady. He decided to change the subject.

'Is Richard Chitfield in fancy dress?' he asked. 'I suppose he ought to be Theseus, Duke of Athens. For here we are at a Court of sorts, and with a wood hard by.'

'What an exciting thought, Sir John!' Mrs Plenderleith, like her husband, was evidently a profound Shakespearian. 'Do you think we shall soon fall into all sorts of confusion?'

'I think it unlikely. This entertainment will no doubt have its muddled moments. But I doubt whether we shall fall into any mystifications ourselves.'

But in this opinion – if, indeed, he held it – Sir John Appleby was to turn out wrong.

VII

There was nothing particularly surprising in the fact that
neither Mark nor Cherry Chitfield had reappeared before
the curtain went up on the Ancient Britons and their bear.
They had dumped Appleby with a vague suggestion that
their father was to be located and introduced to him. But
they had plenty of other things in their heads. And so,
certainly, had Richard Chitfield himself.

The Britons and their bear were quite funny in a
knockabout way. Mrs Plenderleith, with her mind running on Shakespeare, might have remarked that the
creature had been borrowed from *The Winter's Tale* –
with the difference that whereas in the play the bear
chases Antigonus, here the high-spirited young people in
woad chased the bear. Shakespeare moreover is said to
have borrowed an authentic quadruped from the neigh-
bouring bear-garden, while this one would prove in real
life to have only two feet. In fact he was first cousin to the
Teddy bears that had been engaging in archery, and
might even be described as second cousin to the missing
textile tycoon alias Nick Bottom the weaver.

When the curtain came down on the bear-hunt a good
many of the spectators got up and moved around. Experienced in such amateur entertainments, they knew that
some little time would elapse before anything further
happened. Appleby followed their example – cautiously,
since his prime object was to distance himself unobtrusively from the loquacious Mrs Plenderleith. *Ill met* – he
might have been murmuring – *by moonlight, proud
Titania*. Only it was, of course, by sunlight still –
although for that matter it did look as if night might fall

59

before this over-abundant theatrical banquet was over. So Appleby discreetly faded away. He may have been not wholly without thought of that licensed bar, since a mild depression had settled upon him. It was the consequence of a sense that he had set himself a fool's errand. Even if the Chitfield fête did harbour some sort of conundrum, it was no business of his. But now something incipiently enlivening happened. Appleby ran into his fourth sheik.

Not that this was exactly the way of it, for on the present occasion it was definitely a matter of the sheik seeking him out. The sheik, in fact, came up in a hurry, and addressed him without ceremony.

'I say,' the sheik said, 'are you the right Robin Hood?'

'That's hard to know.' Appleby saw instantly that here at last was Tibby Fancroft: an agitated English boy whose pink-and-white complexion was absurdly emphasized by a little black beard stuck slightly aslant on his chin. 'There's certainly another one around, and there may be several. There are undoubtedly a surprising number of sheiks.'

'Yes, it's very puzzling. But what I mean is, are you the Robin Hood who knows Cherry Chitfield? Sir John Somebody.'

'Appleby. Yes, I am. How do you do, Mr Fancroft?'

'Bloody badly. We're fearfully bothered. Or rather Cherry is. So of course I am too.'

'Of course.'

'She told me to find you, and I hope it isn't cheek. You see, Mr Chitfield has disappeared. He's nowhere around the theatre at all.'

'Is that so very alarming? He may simply have been called away about something. I'm told he's very much a man of affairs.'

'Yes, I know. But it's – well, it's unexampled. Cherry says just nothing – or nothing at all normal – would drag him away from this show. Not once it had started, that is. It's so absolutely his thing.'

'So I gather.'

60

'What I myself think is that he's terribly offended. With Cherry and me, I mean. He has seen me in this beastly table-cloth and table-napkin, and gone off in a huff. I thought that, after all, he'd accept the thing as a joke when we actually went through with it. Because, you see, he's jolly decent usually. If I'd known he'd really be cut up I wouldn't have gone ahead. Not even if Cherry –'

'Quite so. But I really don't think that your explanation of Mr Chitfield's absence from the scene is at all a plausible one. He might have done something rather drastic about your silly if harmless desert-lover affair. He might have ordered you out of the place, Mr Fancroft. But he wouldn't withdraw in a sulk. I think you're reading into him – well, a somewhat juvenile attitude of mind. Are you sure, by the way, that he *has* seen you in this get-up?

'Well, no. I've been lying pretty low, as a matter of fact. But somebody says they saw him go off towards the house. So I want to go and apologize to him. I think it would be the right thing. Don't you, sir?'

'Certainly I do.' Appleby spoke as a senior man who has no doubts. 'If you have acted contrary to his expressed wish – however unreasonable it may have seemed to you – here on his own ground and in concert with his own daughter, then you should tell him it was a mistake, and that you are sorry about it. My guess is that it will then all blow over at once.'

'That's what I'm going to do now, Sir John. But I want you to come with me. Or Cherry does.'

'My dear young man, nothing could be more uncalled for or less suitable. I don't know Mr Chitfield. I didn't know *any* Chitfield until yesterday afternoon.' Appleby paused, and remembered how imperiously Cherry had then bidden him to this cluttered-up garden-party-cum-fête. 'Look!' he said abruptly. 'Do you think that Cherry has anything else – perhaps something quite different – in her head?'

'I don't understand.'

'Nor do I, I'm afraid. Does she seem at all worried over something she hasn't told you about? To speak frankly, Cherry seems to me to have her childish side. But she strikes me as a rather sensitive and observant young woman as well.'

'I suppose that's right.' Tibby Fancroft received this by no means unqualified encomium upon his beloved without offence. 'And I have thought her a bit worried about how things are here. I can't think why. Everything seems very nice, to my mind, at Drool Court. And everybody's very nice to *me*. Mrs Chitfield – of course she's of a romantic turn of mind – seems almost to be hearing the wedding bells ringing out merrily already.'

'I'm glad to hear it, Mr Fancroft. And, on second thoughts, I'll come with you to the house.'

There were still plenty of people in the gardens, on the lawns, and besieging the tea-tent. At one end of the terrace the military band still played; it was now dispensing random selections from the treasure-house of Gilbert and Sullivan opera, but at a subdued volume designed not to carry too disturbingly to the theatre at the other end of the grounds. It seemed to be regarded as quite admissible to cut the theatre and amuse oneself in other ways. Appleby had a glimpse of Mr Pring. This particular sheik, no doubt adequately refreshed, was walking composedly up and down between flower beds with his wife. Mrs Pring was taking her part sufficiently seriously to be carrying a somewhat cumbersome banner emblazoned with the Cross of Lorraine. She was a massive woman and – as was to be expected – of maturer years than the Maid of Orleans had been fated to attain.

Appleby wasn't given much time for this further survey. Tibby hurried him on. It appeared that, having been made aware of the impropriety of his conduct in proposing to carry off the younger Miss Chitfield to the tents of the Arabs, he was genuinely anxious to express his regrets to the girl's offended father with as little delay as possible. It was a highly absurd business, and Tibby Fancroft was demonstrably a wholly ingenuous young man. Appleby, who was still quite clear that he himself had no business to be in on the act, accompanied the boy with increasing misgiving.

They entered the house through open doors and an untenanted lobby. Beyond this there was a large hall, in various ways exhibiting signs of affluence. If the Chitfields were really all to be bundled into gaol they would be aware of a painful contrast with their customary surroundings. Nearly everything was in very good taste. Or at least the individual objects deserved that commendation. But in sum they were rather too thick on the ground (or on shelves or in niches and cabinets) for their setting in what was not to be regarded as a formal apartment. Appleby, having cast an appraising eye over various costly trifles, easily to be slipped into a pocket, was surprised by the absence of any sort of guarding presence on such a day as this. Indeed, the whole house had an oddly deserted feel. It was, of course, in no sense open to the public; it was to be expected that the Chitfields would all be out of doors, busy with one or another aspect of the fête; such servants as there might be could well be similarly employed. It was disconcerting, all the same.

'He'll probably be in the library,' Tibby said. 'Come on.'

Appleby failed to see why there should be any probability that Richard Chitfield would be so located, and for a moment he hesitated to come on as required. Indeed, he procrastinated by the first means that occurred to him.

'Has it struck you,' he asked, 'that you ought not perhaps to present yourself to Mr Chitfield in that Arab rig? Your apology might come more gracefully if you got out of it.'

'Oh, I don't know about that.' Tibby had at least come to a halt. 'It's not much more than a bloody white sheet, is it? And that's just right for a penitent.'

This remark, although to be judged unsuitably facetious, at least revealed a glimmer of unexpected intellectual ingenuity on Tibby's part. But Appleby was firm.

'I don't think, Mr Fancroft, that it's at all likely to strike Mr Chitfield in that way.'

'Well, then, it's soon mended. Here goes.' So saying, Tibby plucked the fillet from his brow, raised his arms, ducked his head, and in a moment had wriggled clear of the haik, burnous, or whatever it was that had established him as a desert lover. With a brief yelp of pain, he ripped off his little black beard, and as a result stood revealed as an English youth scarcely out of his teens, dressed in a very commonplace sports-shirt and dark trousers. 'At least it's not at all elaborate,' he said. And he bundled up the whole outfit and tossed it carelessly to the floor. 'Dark glasses, too,' he said; fished a pair out of a pocket, and chucked them on top of the pile. 'I can't think why those wogs think they carry the burning sun of Arabia around with them. And now off we go. The library's the room at the end of the corridor, and quite impressive in its way. I think the books came with the house.'

Appleby was now resigned to what might prove a most unmannerly irruption upon the house's proprietor. But Tibby was behaving with the confidence of one who felt he had the freedom of the place, and with an equal confidence that Richard Chitfield would be found where he supposed him to be. So they marched down the corridor, and halted again at the library door. Quite unmistakably, there came a murmur of voices from within.

'It seems to me,' Appleby said, 'that Chitfield is holding some sort of business conference. And it must be an important and more or less emergency affair to take him unexpectedly away from that cherished theatre. You'd better defer your interview with him, if you ask me.'

'Oh, rot!' Tibby said impatiently and indeed rudely. And he threw open the door and entered the room.

Appleby himself took a couple of paces forward, with the consequence that he became momentarily aware of something very odd indeed. There was a man barring Tibby Fancroft's further progress, and doing so by the decidedly drastic method of pointing a revolver at him. Then a voice spoke sharply from the far end of the room, the revolver vanished, and its owner resumed what was clearly a porter's or guardian's chair by the door.

But if this was disconcerting, the larger spectacle revealed in the library was more confounding still. At one end of a long table was the man who had just briefly spoken: Richard Chitfield, in ordinary clothes, beyond doubt. Facing him at the other end was Nick Bottom the weaver, by no means relieved of the spell that Puck had presumably cast upon him. There were also present the stately sheik of Appleby's earlier observation, a Chinaman, a Teddy bear, the deep-sea diver, and the two bizarrely painted circus clowns.

It might have been expected that Mr Richard Chitfield, an eminently respectable City man, would be a little abashed at being discovered in such odd company. But this wasn't apparently so.

'Tibby,' Mr Chitfield said with mild severity such as might be employed to a son, or the friend of a son, who has committed some minor impropriety, 'you must see that I am engaged.'

'I'm very sorry, sir.' For a moment Tibby Fancroft gaped at the company unbelievingly, much as might a wandering Greek who had strayed into some Circean revel. Then his nerve broke. He turned and fled from the library, unceremoniously bundling a retired Commissioner of Metropolitan Police before him. And the door at once closed behind them, presumably at the hand of its armed janitor.

'Oh, my God!' Tibby exclaimed. 'The place is a bloody madhouse. There can have been nothing like it since the March Hare and the Hatter held that tea-party. Don't you agree, sir?'

'We have certainly glimpsed something a shade on the bizarre side, Mr Fancroft. But we were intruding, after all, and ought not perhaps to complain.'

'I'm not complaining. I'm exclaiming.'

'No doubt. And I'd myself go so far as to join in your pious ejaculation. Oh, my God, as you say. But I don't agree about the bloody madhouse. We have blundered in upon a freak of the imagination, perhaps. But not upon any sort of group lunacy. People don't hold board meetings – for it looked rather like that, wouldn't you say? – togged up as Teddy bears and heathen Chinamen for no better reason than that they ought to be in the bin. The madness has method in it. But whether it's any business of ours, I can't at the moment assert.'

'Not of yours, perhaps. You're here only because Cherry for some reason persuaded you to buy a ticket. But I'm different.' Tibby Fancroft was now contriving to look less bewildered than sulky. 'Cherry's my girl, and I don't think the old chap particularly disapproves of me. Contrariwise, actually. I mayn't be much of a catch, but I have a hunch he'll be quite willing to buy. And that's going to make me part of the Chitfield outfit. And now it proves capable of behaving like this.'

'Perhaps we exaggerate the oddity of the thing, Mr Fancroft. Mr Chitfield's friends and associates come to his party – and in fancy dress, as they have been asked to do. Then the need for a business discussion suddenly turns up, and they get down to it without delaying to change into their London suits and grab their bowler hats and umbrellas. Perhaps it has all been no more than that.'

'You did see that chap with a gun, I suppose? I found myself looking down the bloody barrel of the thing myself.'

'I agree that such a pitch of security is a little odd. But we live in disturbed times. Even the minds of coachmen are unsettled.'

'Funny,' Tibby said gloomily. He was clearly in no mood to receive mild jokes out of Dickens. 'And you don't believe what you're now saying, Sir John. You know that it's unaccountable and alarming, really.'

'Yes, I do.' Appleby had judged Tibby's last speech to be forthright and commendable. 'And now let's get into the open air again.'

The two men were already back in the imposing hall of Drool Court, and they now moved towards the lobby and the open front door. But Tibby Fancroft paused for a moment before walking on.

'I say!' he said. 'Wouldn't that security wallah with the gun be better prowling the house and guarding the family loot? There's a little fortune under our noses at this moment. And the whole place seems deserted. So think what could be stolen just from two or three of the nearer rooms. No end of silver. And even the Boucher! Girl with a perfectly gorgeous bottom. I've sometimes been tempted to pinch her myself. Nobble her, that's to say.'

'Young man, if I understand you aright it is your ambition to enter shortly into the married state. You should endeavour to put licentious thoughts behind you.'

For a moment Tibby appeared disconcerted, and perhaps offended, by this solemnity. It then had the effect, however, of restoring him to a more cheerful mood.

'Arsy-versy on a sofa,' he amplified. 'Would you care to take a quick dekko now, sir?'

'Another time, perhaps. If, that is, I continue to enjoy the acquaintance of the family.' Appleby stepped out on the terrace. 'Are you on fairly intimate terms with Mark Chitfield?'

'Yes, I suppose so. He's not a bad chap, Mark. Succumbed a little too much to education to be quite my sort. But we play squash together, and natter away.'

'Go and find him. Tell him casually about our mild surprise at what we came on in that library, and see if he has anything to say about it.'

'Recruited, am I?' Tibby Fancroft's cheerfulness increased. 'Sexton Blake's boy Tinker, wasn't it? Before my time. But I'll have a go. What about the great sleuth himself?'

'If you mean me, Mr Fancroft . . .'

'Quit Mr Fancrofting me. It's snubby.'

'If you mean me, Tibby, I'm just going to take another walk round.'

'Take care not to loiter in a suspicious manner, sir, or they may nab you.'

'Just who may nab me?'

'Well, it's a funny thing. Although Mr Chitfield doesn't seem to be security-minded about his possessions there in the house, there seem to be a couple of private eyes of a sort prowling the grounds. You could tell them from twenty yards off. And yet what is there to pinch in all that crowd? Nothing except a few bottoms – if that thought may be recurred to.'

'Perhaps they're guarding distinguished visitors.' It had been acute in Tibby Fancroft, Appleby thought, to spot Colonel Pride's mysteriously briefed assistants. Tibby, in fact, was far from being an idiot.

'Let's meet in half an hour in the tea-tent,' Tibby said. 'I'll introduce you to Cherry's mum.'

VIII

The first sight to greet Appleby on emerging from Mr Chitfield's mansion was two more sheiks. Counting Tibby Fancroft (although he had now discarded the character) that made six sighted so far. And these latest recruits were keeping company together; they were engaged, in fact, in what appeared to be conversation of an urgent character, and this was precluding them from taking much notice of their surroundings. But as Appleby now looked down on them from the terrace, it did happen that they both glanced up simultaneously and looked at him. He had a fleeting impression that they didn't much like what they saw – although it was no more than an elderly gentleman dressed up as Robin Hood. Then, whether fortuitously or not, they changed course and moved off towards a corner of the house. Appleby descended a flight of steps and turned in the other direction. He had progressed no more than a dozen paces when yet another couple of sheiks came into view – simultaneously, although they were walking in opposite directions and clearly unconnected with one another. Appleby told himself that these were Pring-like sheiks – which the others just glimpsed in some indefinable way were not.

This throng of desert persons haunting English lawns undoubtedly stood in some need of explanation. Why should it occur to so many men to dress up for Mr Chitfield's fête virtually in an identical way? The most obvious explanation lay in Richard Chitfield himself. He had persuaded his humble associate Mr Pring so to attire himself, and it was conceivable that he had given the same direction to a number of others. But this would have been, surely, a rather pointless joke – in addition to which Appleby had been assured that Mr Chitfield was not of a jocular habit. There was a *serious* reason involved. Appleby was aware that he had known for some time of something serious being afoot at Drool Court. He hadn't, indeed, arrived at Drool as a consequence of quite that knowledge. He had come to the Chitfield fête at the prompting of a fairly trivial curiosity: asking himself why the girl Cherry's father was being so intransigent over the detail of a particular piece of miming or charade. It was now clear, however, that his instinct in this matter had led him into a situation which, although obscure, looked like being far from frivolous. There were two pointers to this. One was the fact that there must be some connection between Richard Chitfield's reluctance to see his younger daughter's suitor dressed up as a sheik and the present plethora of pseudo-sheiks at the somewhat laboured diversion now in progress. The other pointer was the enigmatic instruction or request which had been received by the Chief Constable, Colonel Pride.

It was this last factor that seemed to Appleby to stand most clearly in the way of a quite simple explanation of all those sheiks. Real sheiks were popularly supposed to be possessed, virtually one and all, of almost fabulous wealth. So they were enviable, particularly to persons in the business and commercial sphere in which Richard Chitfield presumably revolved; and as a consequence a number of these – fortuitously and in no sort of concerted manner – had become make-believe sheiks for the afternoon. A similar mechanism had transformed Mrs Pring, for example, into Joan of Arc.

But this wouldn't really do. Appleby knew perfectly well it wouldn't do. There was trouble brewing at Drool Court, and it wasn't of anything that could be called a domestic order. It wasn't at all improbable that some violent event was about to transact itself – and this upon a stage much less confined than that which Mr Chitfield had caused to be erected in a corner of his grounds. An international stage, in fact. One could imagine a thriller based upon it, and appropriately entitled *Seven Sheiks*.

As this thought came to Appleby he rounded a high yew hedge and stopped in his tracks – this with a vivid momentary impression that *Seven Sheiks* would by no means answer. *Twenty Sheiks, Thirty Sheiks*: it looked to be something like that. They were advancing upon him in a solid phalanx, chanting in what was doubtless a ritual Islamic fashion as they came. Then he saw that these were not sheiks but druids. Sheiks and druids, particularly when glimpsed only *en masse*, are capable of resembling one another in a singular degree. And what was here in question was doubtless a local society with bardic interests and unusual astronomical persuasions, making its way to take part in the pageantry of the afternoon. The druids moved with a majestic port. Some of them carried wands. Others walked with raised arms, as if invocating invisible planets. There was a female druid (although this must have been uncanonical, and a concession to the liberated feminism of the age) who was encinctured with what appeared to be plastic mistletoe. The majestic character of the procession, however, was a little marred by the undignified behaviour of a single straggler, who was hurrying forward in the rear while at the same time grappling with his flowing garments as if he had only that moment struggled into them. The main column swung away in the direction of the theatre; the straggler continued to hurry straight ahead; he was quite close to Appleby before Appleby realized that here was not another and laggard druid, but a further sheik after all.

This, in its way, was confusing. To Appleby, however, the spectacle of this scurrying person tugging at his robes at least suggested one small clarification of the perplexed situation at Drool Court. The druids had come through the main entrance to the grounds, as Appleby himself had done on his arrival. And he now remembered that one of the amenities so thoughtfully provided by Mr Chitfield for his guests was located there in a small marquee erected for the purpose. This was where, for a mere five pounds, persons who had not given previous thought to the matter could hire a fancy-dress outfit for the day. Appleby made his way there now.

The inflow of visitors to Drool had almost dried up, and the marquee was deserted except for an elderly woman, a kind of Mistress of the Robes, who sat at a table totting up her accounts. The place smelt strongly of trampled grass and faintly of something like petrol vapour – the latter effect no doubt testifying to the cleaning process regularly undergone by the stock-in-trade of the concern. This was in part arranged in a more or less orderly way on long clothes-racks down one side of the marquee, and in part tumbled about on trestle tables in a forlorn fashion, as if hurriedly and contemptuously rejected by impatient customers. There were several curtained-off spaces, as in a tailor's shop, in which it was presumably possible to robe or disrobe, but no sound came from them. Appleby had the impression that not a great deal of business had been done.

'Good afternoon,' he said, and was aware that there was no reason for a person already dressed up as Robin Hood to penetrate to this curious emporium at all. 'I'm hunting around for a friend who, I believe, may just have arrived, and I thought I might find him here. But I see that I was wrong.'

'I've had only three customers in the last half-hour.' The woman in charge of the place seemed quite willing to converse. 'Things were a little brisker earlier on. But the last of them can't have left more than ten minutes ago.'

'Ah! That may well have been my friend. May I ask what he has got himself up as?'

'As a bedouin. I was rather surprised, as a matter of fact.'

'Surprised, madam?' Appleby's tone was politely curious. 'You wouldn't expect bedouins to be popular? Or sheiks, or persons of that sort?'

72

'Certainly not specially so. But I did include three outfits of that kind in my wardrobe for the day – and suddenly they all went in no time at all. In fact to those last three customers I spoke of.'

'Dear me! They all came in together?'

'Well, no – that's the other curious thing. They came in at intervals of about ten minutes, and with no suggestion that they had anything to do with one another. But I've often noticed that it's funny how a thing will catch on. One lady sees another lady as Madame Pompadour, for instance, or Mrs Siddons, or Helen of Troy, and suddenly thinks she'd cut a more convincing figure as that herself.'

'It's very natural,' Appleby said, 'human vanity being what it is. And that's something your profession must make you aware of, my dear madam. Or so I'd suppose.'

'Certainly it does. And what you say of women goes for men as well. But I can't see why bedouins should suddenly be catchy.'

'It's certainly perplexing. A matter of the warm weather, perhaps. And certainly a wise choice if there is reason to fear a dust storm.' Appleby felt that he had now taken this conversation as far as was useful, and with appropriate murmurs he left the marquee. Simple arithmetic occupied him as he walked back towards the house. Disregard – he told himself – Tibby Fancroft, who as a sheik had retired from the field. Then divide the remaining sheiks into categories. Allow for one *real* sheik (although it was conceivable there wasn't one, and also conceivable that there were more). Allow for three men who decide – suddenly and quite late on in the proceedings – to convert themselves into sheiks on the spot. What remains may be called the Pring group: persons who had arrived at the fête already in the character of desert wanderers – whether or not directly at the prior instigation of their host. Of these Appleby reckoned that there were at least four. The first had been the plump and

73

waddling sheik – who had not been again in evidence. Then there had been Pring himself. And finally there had been the couple almost simultaneously glimpsed but apparently unconnected with one another.

This census was not particularly rewarding, but it did at least suggest that wheels were revolving within wheels at Mr Richard Chitfield's harmless if somewhat heavy-handed frolic at Drool Court. The frolic, incidentally, had largely moved away from the immediate vicinity of the house, which made it seem probable that the theatrical activities were now warming up. To these it was to be presumed that Chitfield himself, being their moving spirit, would hasten back as soon as that peculiar conference in his library was concluded. Appleby felt it to be high time that he had made this enigmatical character's acquaintance. He was about to set off for the theatre, determined to introduce himself without ceremony to his host, when he recalled that he was in fact due to make his bow to his host's wife. So he turned towards the tea-tent instead.

He knew even less about Mrs Chitfield than he did about her husband. On the one hand it appeared that she owned a sound practical sense of the importance, at an affair like this, of what was on offer in the way of food and drink, with the result that she was more concerned with the refreshment marquees than with the theatrical entertainment being so lavishly deployed elsewhere. On the other hand Cherry had awarded her mother the very moderate commendation of being a sensible woman at times, and she had been pronounced by Tibby Fancroft, her hopeful son-in-law to-be, as owning a romantic turn of mind. This was a vague expression, typical (Appleby thought in an elderly way) of a general linguistic impoverishment among the young: a sinister cultural phenomenon to which Professor McIlwraith might devote himself more usefully than to that of phonemic analysis. Tibby had perhaps merely meant that Mrs Chitfield was disposed to look indulgently on love's young dream, and to view him as an eligible suitor for the hand of her younger daughter despite his being without any very obvious means of support.

IX

Tibby Fancroft, although he had jettisoned his garb as a desert lover, hadn't assumed that of a medieval knight in its place. Nobody, after all, would want to spend longer than need be encased – as Cherry had expressed it – like some sardines. And perhaps the episode in which these two young people were to have figured, having proved so much a matter of contention in a family way, had now been tactfully rubbed out of the afternoon's programme altogether. However this might be, Tibby in a minimum of informal attire was more agreeable to the eye – and on a warm afternoon certainly much more comfortable – than the mob of capriciously disguised persons to whom he was helping to dispense tea. (These didn't, Appleby saw with relief, include any more sheiks – nor druids either.)

'Oh, there you are!' Tibby said cheerfully. 'I've told Mrs C. about you, and she's all agog. She'll expect you to tell her about no end of Great Cases of Scotland Yard, and so forth. I've explained to her that it was you who caught Dr Crippen but were baffled by Jack the Ripper. That's right, isn't it? Mrs C., this is Sir John Appleby. Chat him up properly, and he'll keep an eye on the Boucher and all that Chitfield family plate. Particularly on the Boucher.' Having delivered himself – quite inoffensively – of this impudent sally, Tibby dived into the mob and disappeared.

'How do you do?' Mrs Chitfield said. Unlike her husband as glimpsed in his library, she was in fancy dress – although it wasn't of a very readily identifiable sort. Appleby wondered whether she was Cleopatra, that serpent of old Nile: this on the strength of the fact that she had a stuffed serpent of inordinate length coiled round her person. Perhaps, like Rupert and Cynthia Plenderleith (that conjugal Bottom and Titania), she was an ardent Shakespearian. 'You mustn't mind what that Tibby says,' she went on. 'He's a college boy, you know, and they're all like that.'

'Ah, yes. And your son Mark – whom I've had the pleasure of meeting – is a college boy too, of course.' Mrs Chitfield, Appleby concluded at once, had been acquired by Mr Chitfield at an early and modest stage in his social career. 'I've gathered that Mark was a pupil of a new neighbour of mine a couple of parishes away: Professor McIlwraith. And I take it that your elder daughter is a college girl. She talked a little like that.'

'Yes, that's so.' Mrs Chitfield was clearly gratified that Scotland Yard had tumbled to this fact. 'Patience was at Lady Margaret Hall college in Oxford. I found it very confusing at first. There being nobody called Lady Margaret Hall involved at all, I mean.'

'It must be a common misapprehension. May I congratulate you, Mrs Chitfield, on your very becoming dress? I take it you are sustaining the character of –'

'The Cumaean Sibyl,' Mrs Chitfield said (just in time). 'She uttered prophecies, Sir John. Prophecies have always interested me very much. They put us in touch with the Infinite – which is so important, is it not? It's why I have invited the Basingstoke Druids.'

'The Basingstoke Druids?' Appleby repeated, perplexed.

'Yes, the Basingstoke ones. I expect you will have heard of them.'

'Well, no – I can't say that I have. And one would scarcely associate druids with that part of the world.'

'I hadn't heard of them myself until quite lately. But when I invited them to the fête they were delighted to come. There are rather more of them than I expected.'

'They are certainly numerous, Mrs Chitfield. I saw

them arrive, as a matter of fact. In a markedly procession-al manner.'

'Druids are always very processional, Sir John. It's quite a thing with them. And in about half an hour, over in my husband's theatre, they are going to celebrate the Mystery of the Golden Dawn.'

'It sounds most impressive.' Appleby fleetingly wondered what faint bell this information rang in his head. 'But I'm afraid I haven't heard of it either.'

'No doubt it's their special thing. At Basingstoke, you know.'

'No doubt.' Appleby accepted a cup of tea from a passing waitress, and turned back to study the Cumaean Sibyl with some curiosity. He wondered who had told Mrs Chitfield about this celebrated mythological person-age. It seemed improbable that the mistress of Drool was acquainted with Virgil and other prime authorities. He wondered, too, about the relationship of this ingenuous lady to three clever children and a husband who must possess at least a first-rate financial intelligence.

'And later on, at the end of the fête, there is to be a perlustration. I hope you can stay for that. They call it the Perlustration of the House. I'm not quite clear about it, I'm afraid. But I expect it will be very solemn. Perhaps you know what it means?'

'It means another procession, I imagine. All over a territory, or through a building, in a very thorough fashion.'

'That will be it. And with the Asperges. The Asperges are a little extra, it seems, on the bill. But I don't mind the expense at all – not if it adds to some contract with the Higher Unseen. But I don't know quite what they'll *do*.'

'I think it will involve using small brushes on a stick, Mrs Chitfield, to sprinkle water here and there as they move around.'

'I see.' Not unnaturally, the châtelaine of Drool Court received this further information with some misgiving.

'But only a very little,' Appleby added, hastily and

reassuringly. 'Not so as to damage the curtains and chintzes. But I must say that the Basingstoke Druids suggest themselves as rather an eclectic crowd.'

'I suppose it *is* rather eccentric.' Mrs Chitfield sounded a shade offended – having failed quite to gather an incautiously learned word. 'But I felt, you see, that we should touch on a serious note, just at the end. Mark said that it was all going to be very silly – and I wouldn't at all like that to be said about us, not with our position at Drool being what it is. It did occur to me that we might have some Deep Meditation, just before people drive away. But Cherry said people wouldn't be in the mood for it – not when being Teddy bears, and calling themselves Bottom, and that sort of thing. One of Richard's fellow-directors is calling himself Bottom. I think it sounds rather rude.'

'Are many of your husband's fellow-directors and business associates here?' It seemed to Appleby that he'd had enough of the Basingstoke Druids, and that here was an opportunity for cautious exploration in another direction. 'I gather he has important connections pretty well all over the world.'

'Certainly he has.' Mrs Chitfield made this affirmation with a proper pride. 'For a long time, you know, it was sugar. Richard thought he could get all of it.'

'All the sugar in the world?'

'So he said – although I can't think where he was going to keep the stuff. Sugar used to take us to some very nice places – among blacks, of course, but where there was always at least one quite top-class hotel. In the end, however, sugar fell through.'

'Sifted itself away, as it were?'

'Mark used to make that joke, Sir John.' Mrs Chitfield said this without any apparent intention of mild rebuke, but Appleby was nevertheless abashed. 'So Richard went into oil. He said he'd never be more than a small fish in oil. Mark had some joke about that, too, but I've forgotten it. Of course Richard – as you'd know if you knew

79

him – worked himself up quite quickly. That was about the time we bought Drool.'

'So everything was running smoothly. And is it oil still?' As he asked this, Appleby felt that he was bordering upon impertinent – or at least unseasonable – inquisition. But the tea-drinkers were thinning out, and Mrs Chitfield seemed content to continue with family history.

'I'm sure it's mostly oil,' she said. 'But of course there are other things as well. "Interests" is the word for them. Oil has taken us around a good deal too, but mostly in the other direction from sugar. There are some very good hotels on the Persian Gulf. But we haven't been to those parts so much lately, because of revolutions and things of that sort.'

'And do you have many visitors from those parts at Drool? The place seems almost thronged with Arabs this afternoon. But of course they're all just people in fancy dress, which is different. Or nearly all of them are.' Appleby paused on this, but without result. Mrs Chitfield was merely looking vaguely round her.

'No,' she said. 'We don't have many visitors – house-guests, I mean – from foreign parts at all. Richard and his friends have a special house in the country – larger than Drool, I think – where that sort of entertaining is done. We don't go there, the children and I. It's not what you would call a homely place at all.'

'I see. I expect your husband likes to keep his home to himself – except on occasions like this. And he probably doesn't bother you very much with his business affairs.'

'No, and not the children either. You'd expect him to talk to Mark about such things, since Mark is so very clever. But I don't think he ever does. Cherry is his favourite, you know, and I believe he does sometimes talk to her. I've known her be quite worried at times by things he seems to have let fall to her. Isn't that funny?'

Appleby thought that it was at least worth remembering. He also thought that not much more was going to be got out of Cherry's mother, who clearly had a large talent for vagueness over business affairs. It was quite likely, for example, that she was unaware of that emergency meeting (or whatever it had been) which had taken such a bizarre company into her husband's library an hour ago.

'I mustn't monopolize you further,' he said. 'And I think I must make my way to that Mystery of the Golden Dawn.'

'I'll just say a word or two to the caterers, Sir John, and follow you almost at once. You're sure to find Richard at the theatre now, although the people from Basingstoke aren't quite his thing. And I'm certain he'll be delighted to meet you.'

Appleby's own certainty of this was not at all pronounced, but he murmured an appropriate reply before moving away. He himself decidedly wanted to meet Chitfield. And after that it seemed to him that another conference with Colonel Pride would be much in order.

X

But first there was an encounter (which Appleby had known would be inevitable) with the Birch-Blackies. Jane Birch-Blackie had got herself tricked out as a dairymaid of the spruced-up sort to be found in the art of George Morland. Her husband, not at all in the true spirit of fancy dress, had taken it into his head to don his black hunting-coat and buff Bedford cord breeches – thus presenting a most unseasonable appearance to any instructed person who cared to give thought to the matter. Master William Birch-Blackie (shortly to withstand 217 days of siege in an obscure township in Bechuanaland) glowered darkly in his parents' rear. He plainly regarded himself as having been ruthlessly conscripted for this disagreeable duty in the interest of cultivating his father's constituency, and would greatly have preferred to be out shooting rabbits.

'Well, well, my dear John!' Ambrose Birch-Blackie exclaimed with instant cordiality. 'Under the greenwood tree, eh? Tommy Pride, too. Two souls with but a single thought. I'd hardly have expected to see either of you at this show. Where's Judith?'

'Judith's at home, and I've been haled here by one of the daughters of the house. Why Tommy has come, I've no idea.'

'Tommy's a real archer,' Mrs Birch-Blackie said, glancing at Appleby's useless bow. 'I expect he hopes to win a coconut.'

'You don't win coconuts at archery,' William Birch-Blackie said from his retired station and in the special voice employed by children when correcting the ludicrous misapprehensions of their elders. 'Coconuts are at fairs, not fêtes. And fairs are rather better fun.'

'Nice day for the thing,' Ambrose Birch-Blackie said, ignoring this evidence of disaffection. 'I haven't spotted Chitfield yet, or I'd have congratulated him. Big effort, this, and in aid of something or other, of course. I believe it's the Retired Gardeners.'

'Retired Gardeners is at the Brothertons' on Friday,' Mrs Birch-Blackie pronounced decisively. 'This is Distressed Gentlefolk. But Ambrose says we have to go to the Retired Gardeners, too. I'm bound to say we work uncommonly hard.'

'As the gardeners did in their time, no doubt.' Appleby offered this thought with gravity. 'I've never met Richard Chitfield, but I thought I'd introduce myself. Do you know him well, Ambrose?'

'Not exactly. Pass the time of day, and all that. Nice simple wife, with no nonsense to her.'

'Nice and simple, certainly.' Appleby didn't think he could go all the way with the commendation just offered. 'I've run into the three children.'

'Delightful children,' Jane Birch-Blackie said automatically.

'Rubbish, my dear,' her husband said, a shade surprisingly. 'Speak out of turn at the drop of the hat, all three of them. But Chitfield's a decent enough chap of his sort. Stumps up to party funds, and so on.'

'Which I gather he can afford to do.' It had occurred to Appleby that something useful might be got out of this encounter. 'In oil, I hear. Are you in oil, Ambrose?'

'Don't make us laugh,' William Birch-Blackie said outrageously. He had recently been denied promotion from a pony to a hunter, and regarded this as an extreme example of the *res angusta domi*.

'William, cut off. Go and see how the hot-air balloon is getting on.'

'Hot air's about all it is,' William continued on a pertinaciously ungracious note. 'Only last month two men got right across the Atlantic in a balloon and landed up in France. I don't see the point of gaping at a chap soaring skywards from Drool and probably coming smack down on Boxer's Bottom. I'd prefer a Coke to that thrill every time.'

'Then go and get one. There must be gallons of the stuff around.' William's father paused for a moment to watch his son's departure. 'A touch of stage-fright,' he said, as if conscious that his son's comportment was not that predicated of the best type of English public schoolboy. 'William will be absolutely on the ball when his curtain goes up. You'll see. But did you say oil, my dear John? Damned good, that. Half-pay, old boy, and my own three acres and a cow. That's me.' The Birch-Blackies were in fact substantial landowners. 'But my brother, of course, is in with all that City stuff. Knows quite a lot about Chitfield. Some sort of crisis going on, it appears.'

'Chitfield is involved in a crisis?' It seemed to Appleby that his hope was at least in some measure to be fulfilled. 'Connected with oil?'

'That's what my brother seemed to say – and he has been around the Middle East a good deal himself, and knows what he's talking about. Not my territory at all. The Red Sea's bad enough. Ever been to Aden? Jane and I once went round it in a taxi. In the old days and on the way home, that was. P. & O. did coaling there, I expect. Ghastly dump – although it's probably all skyscrapers and Rolls-Royces now. Haven't ever seen any of those little places on the Gulf – nor ever shall now, with Marxists taking over like mad.' Ambrose Birch-Blackie shook his head in a sombre fashion – the picture of a legislator burdened by heavy care. 'Trucial States, and all that – besides no end of places with newfangled names and hoary old corruptions galore. And that's where this Chitfield's trouble lies. Too many oily eggs in one rotten basket, you might say. A lot of those chaps who've been buying up London and a good deal of England as well, you know, pretty well due to be turfed out on their ear.

84

Produces a lot of coming and going in a hush-hush way.'

'A shake-up among the sheiks, in fact.' Appleby had listened with a good deal of attention to all these syntactically imperfect remarks.

'Being gunned for, some of them, on our own doorstep, you might say. Bombs chucked at them as they go shopping in Bond Street. Shocking state of affairs.'

'Isn't it odd,' Jane Birch-Blackie asked, 'that so many people seem to have dressed up as emirs and Arabs and so on this afternoon? It's taking quite a chance, isn't it?'

'They lack imagination,' Appleby said. He was startled by this unusual display of intelligence on the lady's part. At the same time he felt it was desirable to move on, and he cast round for a suitable valedictory remark. 'I look forward,' he said, 'to seeing William put up a really good show against those Boers.'

'He's going to have a capital force under his command.' Ambrose Birch-Blackie had been gratified by this remark. 'I've been to some trouble over it, as a matter of fact. Had to chat up that new OC at Sleep's Hill. But he's done us proud in the way of kit and equipment. A shade anachronistic, perhaps. But the kids aren't going to look like Boy Scouts. Believe you me, you'll take them for a platoon of Guards.'

'Most gratifying,' Appleby said. 'Splendid fun. Goodbye.' And he left the Birch-Blackies to go on their way.

Richard Chitfield, as things now appeared, required more thinking about than Appleby had been inclined to suppose. He was at or near the centre of an obscure affair which was beginning to exhibit a thoroughly sinister appearance. It might be as well to sort all this out a little before tackling the man himself – and only the more so because a retired Commissioner of Metropolitan Police had no business whatever to be nosing round Drool Court in a suspicious – or at least suspecting – fashion. And Chitfield could keep at least for another quarter of an hour. Thus feeling that his present need was for seclusion, Appleby changed course, walked down a long formal garden which was historically quite at odds with the house, went through a gate into the park, and there established himself uncompanionably on a solitary seat beneath an enormous oak. He could still hear faintly the military band on the terrace; and yet more faintly there came to his ear a species of dismal yowling which may have emanated from the Basingstoke Druids as they limbered up to cope with the Golden Dawn. Listening to this for a moment, he realized why there had been something familiar lurking in that phrase. An occult society, active back in the Nineties, had called itself the Order of the Golden Dawn, and various poets of that period had been mixed up with it. But he couldn't recall that it had anything druidical involved. The Basingstoke Druids must just have thought it sounded nice. They were demonstrably a dotty crowd.

But this was by the way, and the present problem concerned sheiks, not druids. So just where did the sheik-business begin?

Chronologically considered, it began with Tibby Fancroft, who had been forbidden to dress up as a desert lover. There was no direct evidence that this had much upset Tibby, but it had upset Cherry Chitfield a good deal. The occasion of her resentment had been entirely childish – but hadn't there lurked in her, distinct from this, some other occasion of disquiet? It appeared that her father had the habit of making her at least fragmentary and sporadic confidences about his affairs, and it was almost as if she had suspected danger or at least mystery in the interdict imposed upon her lover in so arbitrary a way. It was hard to see any other explanation of her sudden wish – childish in itself, no doubt – to have an important policeman around Drool on the occasion of the fête.

It was going to be dangerous to walk around got up as a sheik. At this conception Appleby had arrived already, but he now possessed a larger context within which to consider it. It was perfectly true, as Birch-Blackie had observed, that visitors (or emissaries) to England, alike from the Near East and the Middle East, occasionally carried, as it were, a substantial risk of assassination in their luggage. They were more vulnerable, less easily guarded, in this country than in their own. It could even be a matter of hostile sovereign governments having a go at each other in this way on English soil. And it was, of course, just that sort of hinterland, involving (or thought to involve) delicate diplomatic considerations, that would result in such seemingly absurd assignments as that imposed on Tommy Pride and his token force of two men.

There was at least one real sheik at Drool. This, too, Appleby felt that he knew already. Somehow he hadn't doubted for an instant that his second sheik had been both authentic and important; and he could now again quite clearly call up the image of that hawk-faced man with the stately carriage. Moreover this was the sheik whom he had briefly glimpsed again as present at that confidential confabulation in Richard Chitfield's library in company with the half-dozen of grotesquely disguised persons. This alone set the stately sheik radically apart from the others.

Disguise. Disguise within disguise. Wasn't the real sheik himself to be thought of as disguised, although in a peculiar sense? All the other sheiks were in fact non-sheiks pretending to be authentic sheiks – whether in a blameless fancy-dress way or for reasons less innocent which remained to be determined. But wasn't the real sheik involved in a situation that was considerably more complex? Wasn't he pretending to be in the same boat as the others, supporting – all in the way of fun – a fictitious identity, although in fact he was doing nothing of the kind? He had come to the fête, that was to say, simply as an Englishman who had happened to dress himself up in an Arab fashion. And in this way he had ingeniously made himself into a kind of Invisible Man.

Appleby found himself frowning over this proposition. It penetrated, he believed, well into the target area, but it wasn't too well put. The elaborate exercise he was studying (for elaborate it most certainly was) had really been mounted to *obviate* the real sheik's need to disguise himself. Put it *that* way, and the thing begins to come clear. The sheik is something very grand indeed; perhaps even a monarch. He is a haughty and courageous man, and he abates nothing of these qualities because he is also a threatened man as well. He is not at all minded to huddle into Western clothes in order to elude the observation of his enemies while attending some meeting or conference of high political or financial importance. So what can one arrange? The answer is an improvised additional element in Richard Chitfield's already-planned fancy-dress fête at Drool Court.

Still reposing (in a manner wholly appropriate to Robin Hood) beneath his majestic oak, Appleby assessed this odd sequence of propositions soberly. Perhaps one didn't need to posit anything so sensational as an actual threat of terrorist assassination; perhaps nothing more than confidentiality, the avoidance of publicity essential in the sphere of high finance, was in question. Might not the fact that, with the exception of Chitfield himself, all the other men at that meeting had been heavily disguised have a logical place here? At some tentative stage of large-scale negotiation there might be conferring parties anxious to avoid precise identification for a time. If Chitfield was in danger of being in real trouble (as Birch-Blackie had supposed), and if the authentic sheik was indeed a ruler whose position at home was known to be insecure, there might be good reason why men cautiously considering whether to muck in with them might choose to be unrecognizable one to another.

But what about all the other sheiks? Or, more precisely, what about the two distinct categories of other sheiks?

Richard Chitfield appeared to have indulged some indistinct notion that there was safety in numbers – or safety, at least, for his own important and authentic sheik. So he had seen to it that there would be other sheiks on view. This would account for the Pring contingent. It seemed to imply his belief (which might be justified or not) that such terrorists as were involved would be of a singularly trigger-happy disposition, ready to jump to the conclusion that the first appropriately attired person encountered must be the one they were commissioned to attend to. On this view all these people were seriously at risk. And Chitfield had been concerned that his prospective son-in-law, Tibby Fancroft, should not be among them. A few Prings were another matter. If this had been how Richard Chitfield's mind worked, he was a man quite as ruthless as tycoons of his kind are popularly supposed to be.

And finally there was the other category of pseudo-sheiks: the three men (originally, presumably, in ordinary dress) who had hastily transferred themselves into a further batch of *Arabian Nights* characters at a cost of five pounds per head. For the moment, it had to be admitted, the rôle of these persons was entirely obscure. They might represent, so to speak, reinforcements either on one side or the other. But it was easiest to see them as an enemy within the gates of Drool. The odds were that Richard Chitfield's elaborate manœuvre was in danger of failure, as many elaborate manœuvres turn out to be. The whereabouts of the all-important authentic sheik had become known to his adversaries. And they were here on the spot.

XI

Appleby's train of thought, as thus briefly summarized, might have entirely pleased a detective intelligence less experienced than his own. As far as it went, his picture of the mysterious affair at Drool hung together well enough. But it was no more than a hypothesis, and the problem now was to find some means of subjecting it to verification through experiment. The person to whom to apply this technique was certainly Richard Chitfield. To Chitfield Appleby must, as he had planned, introduce himself; and he must then chat briefly in the most harmless way before suddenly springing so knowledgeable-seeming a question that the chap would be surprised into spilling any beans that he happened to be carrying round in his pocket: for example, the identity of the authentic sheik.

Primitive guile of this sort was part of the policeman's stock-in-trade, and it was remarkable how often it worked. On the present occasion, however, the investigation went ahead for a time along different lines. This was a result of the reappearance of Colonel Pride, who had spotted Appleby under his oak and was now hurrying towards him. From afar their meeting might have been judged a wholly Arcadian encounter of the homespun English order. Here were two jolly outlaws in Lincoln green planning a little deer-stealing or the like at the expense of an overweening local magnate.

'Glad to spot you, John,' Pride said. 'They've taken the wraps off. Message just come through. The "over to you" sort of thing.'

'Just who have taken the wraps off?'

'Those leather-bottoms at the FO, of course. Ghastly life they seem to have. Never stand up, except to drink tomato-juice at cocktail-parties. My father was in that outfit, you know. But he warned me off the Diplomatic when I was quite a kid. Sensible of him. Shoved me into the Brigade instead, and there I was when the *Führer*'s bloody curtain went up. Fortunate thing. Do you know that the feminine of *Führer* means a bus conductress? Poor old Adolf never thought of that one.'

'I suppose not.' Appleby conjectured that some state of obscure excitement was responsible for these random autobiographical excursions on Tommy Pride's part. 'And just what has the Foreign Office taken the wraps off?'

'What's cooking at Drool – or what they've been thinking may be cooking at Drool. It's all about a fellow called an emir. Now, what would you say an emir is?'

'My new neighbour, Professor McIlwraith, would tell you that it's the same word as Admiral. But it can be a title of honour borne by the descendants of Mohammed, or it can mean simply a prince. Not quite a top-drawer prince, perhaps. I seem to recall Gibbon recording that the humble title of emir was no longer suitable to the Ottoman greatness.'

'Is that so? Remarkable thing.' Colonel Pride was accustomed to his friend Appleby sometimes exhibiting a professorial side himself. 'Well, this chap, who's called the Emir Afreet –'

'Are you sure of that, Tommy? It sounds most improbable. An afreet is an evil demon or monster.'

'Well, that's what my man in the car park took it down as on his radio blower affair. It's not important. The point is that the chap's here at this confounded jamboree.'

'So he is, Tommy. And rather impressive, although not particularly demoniac.'

'Ah, yes.' For a moment the Chief Constable had received this information without surprise. But quickly his features expressed a natural bewilderment. 'You know about him already?'

'Well, at least I've seen him. And I imagine your friends at the Foreign Office believe him to be under some sort of threat. Of assassination, say. Or perhaps merely of kidnapping. He's rather rash, you see. Perhaps "intrepid" is the worthier word. Not at all disposed to hide himself behind a massive bodyguard, or even get himself into unobtrusive Western-style togs. Particularly when he has a big deal on hand with fellows like Chitfield and his associates. I think they may be trying to rescue each other – Chitfield and the Emir – from some ticklish political and financial corner.'

'You seem to know a lot more about this Arab than I do.' The Chief Constable was staring at Appleby much as Dr Watson had been habituated to stare at a Sherlock Holmes in full deductive spate. 'Perhaps you can tell me where to find him.'

'I could have told you where to find him an hour ago. But I haven't a clue as to where he is now. On his way back to London, perhaps.'

'I damned well hope so. But I suppose we must look around. A fellow dressed up from the family wash-basket oughtn't to be too difficult to spot.'

'My dear Tommy, haven't you noticed? One emir- or sheik-like character has recently retired from the field in the person of a certain Tibby Fancroft. But there is a minimum of eight others still enjoying the fun. Mind you, I could myself pick out the real one from quite a distance away. But the position holds possibilities of some confusion, all the same. And what are you meant to do about the Emir Afreet, anyway? Bundle him into his Rolls and tell the chauffeur to drive him back to town? It's just conceivable that he might regard you as taking something of a liberty. And the FO wouldn't care for that at all.'

'Confound the Foreign Office – and the Home Office as well. I'm asked to keep things under observation, and act only in an emergency.'

'I've heard that one before.' It was obvious that Appleby didn't think highly of it. 'Are your two men armed, Tommy?'

'Of course they're not armed!' The Chief Constable was scandalized. 'Where do you think we are, my dear John: the streets of Chicago?' Although there was nobody within a couple of hundred yards, he cautiously lowered his voice. 'Although, as a matter of fact, I do carry a little toy affair myself.'

'Well, why not? I don't think I'd suspect you of being a trigger-happy type. But some of those pseudo-sheiks may be.'

'What do you mean, John – pseudo-sheiks?'

'It's like this. As well as your Emir, there are at least seven men dressed up as Arabs at this party. And I do mean *dressed up*. Not one of them could sit a camel, or would know how to enter a mosque. But they divide into two groups. Four of them are, I think, minor associates of Chitfield's, and at least one of them is here dressed as he is at Chitfield's direct suggestion.'

'That's uncommonly odd.'

'Yes, it is. But remember how medieval kings would dress up half a dozen unfortunate fellows exactly like themselves – crown and all, no doubt – and shove them into the battle to bamboozle the enemy. It's something like that. The other group is a trio – and all three of them have simply turned themselves into Arabs at short notice with the aid of stuff that can be hired near the main gate.'

'Why ever should they do that? And is Chitfield at the bottom of this ploy too?'

'I'm pretty sure that Chitfield knows nothing about it. But your first question, Tommy, I can't answer at all.'

'I suppose it's natural that you should preserve a scrap of ignorance here and there.' The Chief Constable produced this sally with considerable satisfaction. 'Is there anything else that it would be only kind to apprise me of?'

'Only that you were quite right in suspecting a high-level hinterland to the whole affair. A ruler, or a

93

government, in your Emir's part of the world in danger of toppling, and Chitfield and his crowd likely to tumble with them. That kind of thing. Fishing in troubled waters – but with no shortage of oil to pour on them.' Appleby paused expectantly on this witticism – which, however, the Chief Constable was too preoccupied to appreciate. 'All, of course, comparatively small fry. Chitfield's middle name isn't exactly BP or Shell. But the affair is big enough to be of international concern.'

'Puts us on our toes, eh?' Colonel Pride suddenly chuckled happily. 'I'm relieved, you know, about one thing. I had that notion of being involved in a thoroughly discreditable show. Letting *A* damn well mow down *B* if he wanted to, but with a vague suggestion that somebody was around trying to keep the Queen's peace. There's a lot of that sort of no-holds-barred stuff nowadays.'

'Mostly in thrillers, my dear Tommy. And you're quite justified in concluding it's not that kind of thing on the present occasion. You locate the Emir, and protect him as effectively as you can without anybody remarking the fact. Probably – and quite apart from the personal intrepidity stuff – he wouldn't like it to be known at home that he required the protection of the British police.'

'Don't you think he may tote around an unobtrusive bodyguard of his own?'

'Yes, I do. I've got my bearings in all this, as a matter of fact, partly from having blundered in on a kind of directors' meeting earlier in the afternoon. There was the Emir, and there was Chitfield, and there were half a dozen other people too. But there was also a fellow with a gun. Whether he was the Emir's property, or Chitfield's, I wouldn't know.' Appleby stood up from his seat beneath the oak. 'I suppose we'd better be getting back on the beat.'

For a short space the two men walked in thoughtful silence, and then it was Pride who first spoke.

'So just what now?' he asked.

'I do my best to locate the Emir. It may be, of course,

that having concluded his business with the Chitfield crowd, he has driven, as I suggested, straight back to London. But somehow I don't think so. For I have this impression that he is a pretty regal character, and that notions of courtesy would require him a little to partici-pate in – or at least view – the entertainments on offer before making off. Particularly if he's anxious to give the impression of being able to move about England quite securely. So, as I say, I do my best to find him. I then tip you off about him, and you tip off your two men – supposing you're able to find them. Between them they need never be far away, quite without his tumbling to their identity. And you remember that trio of pseudo-sheiks? It's a long shot, but I do in an obscure and groping way see them as a point of danger. Were they suddenly to converge on the Emir, that would be the moment to look out for the daggers. Quite like Julius Caesar on the Capitol – particularly with the whole lot of them giving that laundry-basket effect.'

'I wonder whether it would be discreet to have a word with Chitfield? John, what do you think? He might well take offence at discovering I was prowling around here in this absurd pantomime dress, and that I had a couple of Dicks on the premises without so much as a by-your-leave.'

'I think you're right. Better leave it to me. I've been invited to this nonsense by his favourite child, you know – so I can't easily be taken exception to. But first things first. Hunt the Emir.'

XII

On this occasion Appleby had barely parted from Colonel Pride when he was accosted by Professor Mc-Ilwraith. The eminent philologist, indeed, appeared to have been in two minds as to which of these police-manly characters he wanted to address. And when he spoke it was to reveal a surprising state of perturbation.

'Sir John,' he said abruptly, 'I must know, please, whether you are present at this absurd affair in an official character.'

'No, I am not.' Appleby was considerably astonished by this brusque demand. 'I thought I'd made that clear when we ran into one another. I was simply invited to come along by Cherry Chitfield.'

'And that man – that other Robin Hood – who has just left you? I gathered that he is the Chief Constable of the county. Is that so?'

'Well, not exactly of the county, any longer. But that's the general idea. Colonel Pride.'

'Is Colonel Pride here officially?'

'My dear sir, I can tell you nothing about Colonel Pride.' Appleby's surprise had increased, and he felt that he had perhaps spoken more stiffly than was required. He was certainly not entitled to give this slightly dotty scholar any information about Tommy Pride, nor had he any immediate impulse to be more communicative about himself than he had been. On the other hand, Mc-Ilwraith's odd state of mind appeared to require expla-nation, and merited as much investigation as any of the other current puzzles at Drool. So Appleby spoke again.

'Has anything happened to disturb you, Professor? Can I help you in any way?'

'That young man called Fancroft, Sir John.' McIlwraith had now a little composed himself. 'Mark Chitfield has told me a very disconcerting yarn about him. Unfortunately it is often impossible to tell when Mark is romancing and when he is not.'

'That I can well believe.'

'The story is that Fancroft was anxious for some trivial reason to appear at this fête in Arab costume, and that Richard Chitfield forbade him to do so in the most peremptory fashion. I am aware that you don't know any of these people particularly well, Appleby. But have you any reason to believe that this is true?'

'Yes, I have. It is almost certainly true.' Appleby produced this reply at once. He was suddenly convinced that McIlwraith was in some way bound in with whatever design was at present weaving itself at Drool Court, and that it was desirable to encourage him to talk. 'And it seems,' he went on, 'that there is an explanation of sorts – what might be called an ostensible explanation – connected with the afternoon's theatrical activities. Cherry has wanted to be a modern English girl carried off by a desert lover, and her father has judged that to be indelicate. He has wanted her to be a medieval maiden, rescued by a knight from a dragon or a sorceress or something of the sort. What do you make of that, McIlwraith?'

'Absolute nonsense!'

'Quite so.'

'My dear Appleby, I must confide in you.' Professor McIlwraith took a cautious glance around him. 'The true explanation –'

'The true explanation is that some serious risk attends being dressed up as an Arab at Drool this afternoon, and that our host didn't want his daughter's young man to be exposed to it. So much I can make out for myself. But your attitude makes me feel you know more about it all than I do. And as I am in a sense taking a professional interest in what's going on, I'll be glad to hear anything you have to say. For instance, perhaps you can tell me why the place is stuffing with fellows dressed up as Arabs. It's a fact that can scarcely have escaped your observation.'

'It has not. And I imagine it hasn't escaped your speculative instincts either.'

'True enough.' Professor McIlwraith, Appleby thought, was turning a little less pedantic than usual, which was perhaps a good sign. 'I posit at least one genuine Arab, who is the person actually under threat. The imitation Arabs have been brought in to confuse matters. You might call them extra needles chucked into the haystack.'

'That's the only possible explanation of them?'

'Far from it. There may be more than one category of imitation Arab. Somebody may have decided that, having taken our thought so far, we shall think of all imitation Arabs as necessarily harmless. We shall judge them either to be in Arab costume purely fortuitously – which is perfectly possible – or to be among the spare needles, and therefore necessarily without any lethal intentions.'

'My dear Appleby, that, if I may say so, is a most refined analysis. I congratulate you.'

'I don't want congratulations.' Appleby was suddenly impatient. 'I want facts. If I read your mind rightly, you are as apprehensive as I am that some serious threat hangs over this blasted fête. So I think we'd better pool our information. For my part, I've told you all I know.'

'Except about your colleague Colonel Pride.'

'Perfectly true. But you must tackle him yourself. He's fair game enough. But you and I can start with the real Arab. I've been thinking about him as Sheik somebody. But now I have some reason to think of him as an emir. Emir Afreet, as a matter of fact.'

'My dear Appleby, an afreet is –'

'Yes, I know. But that's how it came over on a telephone.'

'Is it, indeed?' Very naturally, Professor McIlwraith gave this information a moment's thought. 'A telephone message to Pride?'

'To one of Pride's men. There's a police presence here, although a regrettably small one. It's only wise to tell you that.'

'I see.' McIlwraith gave this intelligence brief consideration in turn. 'Emir Hafrait is the name of the man who has come to Drool. You may well have heard of him, Appleby. He's a fellow of considerable importance in his way. And the occasion of my being here myself, as a matter of fact.'

'Ah! Now we're getting somewhere.'

'Not very far, I fear. The Emir is here for extremely confidential discussions with Chitfield and his associates over oil revenues and so on.'

'I'd imagined as much.'

'It's stuff with which I have nothing to do. But I am Hafrait's adviser on other matters. They may be called religious matters.'

'Dear me!' Appleby was genuinely astonished. 'I'd have thought –'

'Quite so. But during my long period in the Middle East I made, as it happens, a fairly searching study of Islam. It isn't, you know, all that monolithic. In fact you never know in what direction this or that Mohammedan cat will jump. Hafrait's is a modern and purely secular mind, and he finds it useful that I can offer him a wholly dispassionate view of the warring sects and their political implications. I was to have some discussion with him this afternoon when his commercial concerns were concluded. But now he has disappeared. And that is why I am holding this conversation with you.'

'Ah, yes.' Appleby didn't quite know what to make of all this. It didn't sound too plausible, but was certainly not to be ignored. 'Supposing,' he went on, 'that your

Emir really is under some actual threat – as I may say I'm inclined to accept, since all this hush-hush business would be pointless otherwise. Does the threat come from a purely political quarter – the toppling of one ruler in favour of another – or is it a matter of what is called Big Business in a particularly ruthless aspect, or is the motive one of religious fanaticism – as your last remarks would appear to suggest?'

'My dear Appleby, you can know little of the Middle East if you believe that there is any separating all that. Search for the motive prompting any action between Suez and Tehran, and nothing but a mishmash confronts you. You wouldn't care for it, my dear Appleby. It must make complex detective investigation very difficult. But of course the solving of criminal problems is on the whole simply conducted. You simply choose a suitable suspect and find some appropriate means of making him say what you want him to.'

'I'm afraid you and I would meet with a certain amount of disapproval if we went to work that way.'

'Decidedly we should. But we must get to work *some* way. I must say, Appleby, that I am displeased with Chitfield. His attitude over the ridiculous Fancroft shows that he has been well aware of the hazardousness of Hafrait's coming to Drool at all. And he has dealt with the matter in a wholly freakish and irresponsible manner.'

'I'm inclined to agree with you there, McIlwraith. We'd certainly better find your Emir, and find Chitfield as well – and get the whole dangerous business wound up as soon as may be.'

'Quite so.' Professor McIlwraith appeared to find encouragement in this brisk assumption that dangerous businesses are by their nature amenable to swift control. 'Perhaps we'd better separate and scour the place. But would you know Hafrait if you saw him?'

'I rather imagine I'd know him instantly. I've had a couple of sightings, you know: once here in the grounds, and once in the library. Tall and commanding – and even his dark glasses don't obscure the fact that he looks like an eagle – as emirs no doubt should.'

'Or like a vulture.' McIlwraith seemed to offer this alternative as a man well up in Middle East affairs.

'And Chitfield's pseudo-sheiks, as I've been thinking of them – a little chap called Pring and the others – don't come within anything like a foot of him. Decidedly a tall man of his hands, your Emir. What, by the way, makes you say so roundly that he has disappeared?'

'Simply that he was to remain in the library after Chitfield had got rid of his associates and their business with Hafrait – whom I was then to join there. But he'd vanished. Chitfield too, for that matter.'

'It appears to be a general opinion that Chitfield is likely to have gravitated to his precious theatre – although it looks as if he may well have been distracted from all that nonsense. I suggest that we scour around separately, and meet up there in, say, fifteen minutes. But if you run into Pride, you'd better spare a little time to explaining yourself. There's too much haphazard about all this at present. Rather more in the way of liaison is distinctly called for.' Appleby let a good deal of personal disapproval percolate through this remark. 'Whatever the threat is, I'd like to feel surer than I do that we have an adequate force to cope with it.'

'Dear me!' Professor McIlwraith said. 'I am much to seek, I fear, at this sort of thing. But as your faithful Achates, my dear Appleby, I shall do what I can.'

XIII

The Emir Hafrait, having concluded his business with what might be thought of as Chitfield's crowd, had failed to remain in that library for the purpose of seeing Professor McIlwraith – or for the purpose, perhaps one ought to say, of receiving Professor McIlwraith. No doubt (Appleby told himself as he began his prowl) this was a circumstance less significant than McIlwraith imagined. Hafrait was probably the next thing to royalty, and if it pleased him to wander off and take a look at his client Chitfield's bizarre entertainment, he might very well judge it the obscure McIlwraith's business to hang around and await his better leisure. Appleby, in fact, was rather clinging to his notion of an intrepid aristocratic Arab going his own way. The fellow might, of course, have his own effective security around him in a manner unknown even to his host of the afternoon. After all, anybody could be pretty well anything in this fancy-dress crush.

And the crush was still increasing. Appleby was again astonished that such a very large number of presumably rational beings should choose to put in a long and exhausting afternoon at the Chitfield fête. Into an open-air party it is no doubt entirely lawful to cram as many human bodies as you please, but if you had a roof over the heads of this crowd no fire-prevention people would tolerate the spectacle for a second. And it certainly made Appleby's present occupation peculiarly difficult; the sheer compactedness of the haystack made the hunt-the-needle business distinctly unpromising. And now he became aware of an additional obstacle. As he had already observed, sheiks and druids, unless viewed at close quarters, are much of a muchness, and he found himself repeatedly mistaking the one for the other. The Basingstoke contingent, having presumably despatched the ritual of the Golden Dawn, and having some time to spare before the yet more solemn ceremony of the perlustration of Drool Court, were recreating themselves severally or in small groups by wandering round the less arcane entertainments on offer. And as one or two of them were exceptionally tall, Appleby once or twice found himself imagining that he was about to run the Emir Hafrait to earth when in fact he was doing nothing of the sort. But then – quite suddenly – there the real chap was. Here, most definitely, was not another Pringtype pseudo-sheik. It was impossible to mistake that regal port.

Sir John Appleby, being a well-trained policeman, glanced at his watch, and then made a dive for his quarry. But it had to be a little more than a dive. Richard Chitfield's distinguished guest was plainly occupying himself in the manner Appleby had judged probable; much like the druids, he was taking a walk round the sights. And now he was standing at the other side of a tight ring of spectators surrounding the hot-air balloon as it laboriously puffed itself into shape. By the time Appleby had circumambulated this mob, the man had vanished. Surely it couldn't be that he had become aware of the fact that a retired Commissioner of Metropolitan Police, absurdly dressed up as Robin Hood, was about to have the impertinence to accost him? No, it couldn't be that. It was merely that, by very bad luck, the Emir Hafrait had chosen to move on to the next idle attraction.

Even so, he was so tall that it ought to have been possible to distinguish his head bobbing away in one direction or another. But this wasn't the case. Some configuration of the terrain must be preventing it. There was nothing to do but continue to move towards the theatre. The theatre was, after all, the centre-piece of the whole jamboree. It was the likeliest place for the Emir himself to be making for, even if circuitously, just as it was the likeliest place at which to effect the almost equally desirable running to earth of Richard Chitfield. But as either of these elusive characters might be almost anywhere else about the place, Appleby now went forward slowly and looking around him – rather like any less exalted policeman on the beat in some shady district. As a consequence of this it took him some time to arrive back at the theatre.

As on the previous occasion, little was happening. There was nothing very surprising about that. What was perhaps unexpected was the large number of persons sitting in patient expectation of whatever might be the next event. This could be because a period had arrived in the afternoon's proceedings at which people were relieved simply to be able to get off their feet. There was, indeed, a certain bustle in what was at least theoretically behind the scenes – occasioned by William Birch-Blackie and his companions limbering up to defend Mafeking to the death. There was no sign of any Boers. These ought, roughly speaking, to have been recruited from the surrounding juvenile peasantry of Drool. Perhaps they had refused to play. Or perhaps nobody had remembered that Boers were necessary.

Appleby glanced at the spectators. Titania was present, and this time Bottom (last glimpsed in Richard Chitfield's library) had been restored to her. Sheik Pring was also on view, with Joan of Arc seated incongruously beside him. But now this more or less static scene was broken into by what was at least the ghost of an event. Professor McIlwraith, already arrived at this agreed rendezvous, had spotted Appleby and was advancing upon him at a lumbering run.

'I've seen him!' McIlwraith called out in an agitated manner. 'He has been here. But now he has disappeared again.'

'Do you mean the Emir?' Naturally enough, Appleby disapproved of this public display of perturbation.

'Yes, of course. Only ten minutes ago.'

'Ten minutes ago?' Appleby was astonished to see that the eminent philologist had glanced at his watch. 'You thought to note the actual minute you spotted him?'

'Certainly I did. I hurried straight here, you know. And there Hafrait was – strolling about as if he were at a garden party.'

'Well, he was – wasn't he?' Appleby felt a moment of sheer exasperation. 'Confound it, McIlwraith! I think there be six Richmonds in the field. That's all that can be said about it.'

'Just what do you mean by that?'

'I mean that Hafrait – unless he really is an afreet into the bargain – can't be in two places at the same time. And I could swear I saw him ten minutes ago in quite a different corner of the grounds. How certain are you that your man really was the Emir?'

'Totally certain. He spoke to me. And in rather a high-handed manner, I'm bound to say. You see, we had an appointment –'

'Yes, I remember about that.'

'Well, he simply waved at me – and said, "Our occasion must be a little later, my good McIlwraith." And then he moved away. I let him go. I was too annoyed to endeavour to detain him.'

'That was very natural, no doubt. The fact is that the fellow is showing off, isn't it? He's amusing himself with a kind of variant on Russian roulette. He's here, together with some unfortunate double he has brought along with him, and it's fifty-fifty which of them cops it. The thing is absolutely dotty.'

'They are a peculiar people, my dear Appleby. It is my conjecture that Hafrait was offended when he heard of Chitfield's inept plan to have other persons in Arab costume around – and the result has been even more irrational behaviour on his own part. In face of such nonsense, I hardly see we can do other than throw in our hand.'

'It might be the sensible thing, I agree. But one can't, unfortunately, contract out of a duty to endeavour to keep the Queen's peace. In particular, Colonel Pride and his men can't. We must put Pride wise to this new development at once.'

Professor McIlwraith appeared properly impressed by this elevated view of the matter.

'I am constrained to agree with you,' he said. 'And we must act simply as if we were concerned to break up a rough house in a pub.' McIlwraith paused, perhaps in surprise at having arrived at this unassuming comparison. 'One simply separates the parties; tells them to give over and clear off.'

'Quite so. But in the present situation the Emir himself is the only party we are in a position to deal with. And I somehow don't think much would come of our asking him to quit the field – even supposing we can find him again. He's showing off, as I've said. And he won't be disposed to take orders from anybody to leave Drool.'

'Except, perhaps, from Chitfield. He no doubt regards Chitfield as a servant, just as he does me. But, on this particular occasion, Chitfield is also his host. Hafrait would not care to remain here as a formally unacceptable guest. He might turn nasty later. But at the moment, he'd go.'

'Then Chitfield must be persuaded of the necessity of having a shot at just, that. Unfortunately Chitfield appears to be quite as elusive as the Emir. You've seen no sign of him back-stage, or whatever the expression is?'

'No, I have not. And I continue to feel that he has been behaving in a thoroughly vexatious manner.'

'Possibly so. But he may –' Appleby, who had been scanning the middle distance as he spoke, broke off suddenly. 'But here is his elder daughter, apparently coming up from the archery field. And looking for somebody. It's a disposition that seems to be catching.' Appleby continued to watch Patty Chitfield as she approached. 'McIlwraith – do you know? I have a notion something has happened.'

'I told my father you were here, and he asked me to find you.' Miss Chitfield had addressed Appleby briskly, and with only a glance at his companion. 'We've found a doctor, but we need a policeman too.'

'Then it isn't me you want, but –' Appleby checked himself. It was still no business of his to disclose to all and sundry the presence of Colonel Pride. 'I noticed a constable with a Panda car at the main gate,' he emended. 'Guiding the traffic, I suppose. If something has happened requiring the police, he's the proper man to get hold of.'

'In that case we'll have to have you improperly, Sir John. This is something quite urgent. Please come to the archery ground at once.'

'Very well.' Appleby was in fact without any serious intention of taking a stand on the proprieties. 'Has there been an accident there?'

'It would be better to call it an incident. Somebody has been shot.'

'I see. Might he be described as a wandering Arab, Miss Chitfield?'

'Certainly he might.' Patty gave Appleby a queer glance. 'At least it isn't Tibby Fancroft.'

'Quite so. And I think that perhaps Professor McIlwraith – you know Professor McIlwraith? – had better come along too.'

'Of course I know him.' Patty favoured the philologist with a quick nod. 'Now, for goodness' sake, get moving.'

The three were in fact already moving, so Patty's brusque injunction suggested that she was considerably upset. Appleby, although reflecting that, if there was a doctor already on the scene, the next urgent requirement must be an ambulance rather than a policeman, was quite willing to hurry. And here no crush impeded them; it looked as if the actual archery competitions had been wound up and everybody had gone off elsewhere. In fact there was only a single small group of people to be seen. They were congregated beside one of the targets on the nearer side of the range. And in the middle of them, huddled on the ground, was a figure swathed in white. It reminded Appleby grimly of that joke about a laundry basket.

There was a uniformed policeman – so somebody else must have remembered about the Panda car. There was a man who could be spotted as the doctor, although he was got up to look like Robinson Crusoe. Mark Chitfield and Tibby Fancroft were standing side by side – the latter still in the sports shirt and trousers to which he had stripped outside Richard Chitfield's library. And there was Chitfield himself, who swung round at the approach of the new arrivals.

'Here is Sir John Appleby,' Patty said rather baldly. She had glanced at her father and appeared to dislike what she saw. This was not altogether unreasonable. For a master of high finance – or whatever he was – Mr Chitfield was for the moment cutting an unimpressive figure. To declare that he was panic-stricken would have been to observe a decent moderation in speech.

'He's dead!' Chitfield said hoarsely. 'Hafrait's dead. If it gets known – that he died here – the whole thing will crash.' He glared at Appleby, who received this mildly surprising and not very decent view of the matter impassively. Mark Chitfield, although very pale, failed to resist raising his eyes to heaven as if to acknowledge a consciousness that for the whole Chitfield family the prison gates were about to gape open at last. Tibby seemed entirely bewildered. And Appleby noticed for the first time that he was a tall youth – almost as tall as the Emir Hafrait. It looked as if, had he *not* shed that Arab garb, he might have been decidedly at risk.

'Dead!' Chitfield reiterated, and swung round towards the doctor. 'He *is* dead? You're sure of it?'

'He is most certainly dead.' The doctor, who had been obliged to set down on the grass a palm-leaf umbrella and an ancient fowling-piece, stooped and retrieved these absurd objects composedly. He was a local man, and as he did so he recognized Appleby, who was still carrying around his equally absurd long-bow. 'Good afternoon, Sir John,' he said. 'Rather your sort of thing, I imagine. Or a very peculiar accident, to say the least. Take a look.'

Thus bidden, and under the respectful gaze of the constable, Appleby stepped forward and obeyed this injunction. The body was lying on its side. It was so lying because it could not have been very decently disposed in any other fashion. The arrow – for it had been a bow-and-arrow affair – had entered from behind. A third of it, the feathered third, protruded between the shoulder blades. Another third, the barbed third, similarly protruded from the chest. The final third was inside the dead man. There was little doubt that surgery would be required to remove it.

'Chitfield, you are a fool!' It was Professor McIlwraith who produced this unseemly exclamation. He had advanced, knelt down, and peered closely and without ceremony at the dead man's face. 'They haven't killed the Emir, but some fellow unfortunate enough to look like him. Not a spurious Arab, like your absurd Pring, but a member of his own entourage, given the nasty job of taking the risk.'

'Of sharing the risk,' Appleby said. 'You have to give your tiresome Emir that. Russian roulette again. He has a taste, in fact, for a decidedly drastic form of gambling. McIlwraith, what is your opinion of all this?'

'That it mayn't take them long to discover their mistake. If Hafrait is indeed strolling round this wretched fête with a full knowledge of the risk he runs – and it's entirely in the man's character, I'm bound to say – then a single close-up glimpse of him, upright on his two feet, will tell these assassins just how they've been fooled. And when that happens they will presumably go to work again.'

'Perfectly true.' Appleby turned to Richard Chitfield. 'I know nothing about the merits of this Hafrait as a business associate,' he said drily. 'But he is quite plainly a most undesirable guest. I advise you to get rid of him.'

'But not in too summary a fashion,' Mark Chitfield said with unsuitable cheerfulness. And he glanced down at the dead man. 'That's been tried already.'

XIV

'One possibility occurs to me,' Professor McIlwraith said. This odd scholar, Appleby reflected, seemed curiously unperturbed by the horrific spectacle almost at his feet. His academic career had perhaps not been of a uniformly sheltered kind; spells of duty even as a scholar in Tehran and similar places might well have inured him to running up against violent situations at one time or another. 'Although, as I have already mentioned, the Emir thought fit to treat me in a somewhat cavalier fashion earlier this afternoon, there are undoubtedly certain matters of a quasi-political sort upon which he is designing to consult me. And now – having, so to speak, done the honours of the fête and thereby played his foolish roulette – he may simply have returned to the house and be expecting me to be at his disposal in the library. I suggest that we investigate that possibility.'

'If he has done anything of the sort,' Appleby said, 'it strikes me that he may have placed himself in quite as unguarded a situation as when he was wandering around the grounds. When Mr Fancroft led me to your library, Mr Chitfield – and incidentally to a glimpse of a singular-ly bizarre meeting – it struck me that the house and its contents were notably vulnerable to petty, or not so petty, theft. There seemed to be nobody about at all. Except, indeed, that your meeting itself was guarded by a man with a revolver. He directed it, until checked by you, upon Mr Fancroft and myself. Is he to be described as a personal guard of your own?'

'Yes, he is. But that doesn't signify.'

'It certainly seems to signify, sir, a certain disregard of

the law. The circumstances in which such a person is entitled to carry firearms are very rare indeed. But we needn't, at the moment, pause over that. This officer' – and Appleby nodded towards the constable – 'will see to it that the Chief Constable is contacted and the proper procedures in relation to this dead man put into effect. I think the younger people may usefully assist in finding him. He is, as you may already know, the other Robin Hood. You and I, Professor, will go with Mr Chitfield to the library, where we may perhaps find this tiresome potentate as you suggest.'

In this simple way, without authority and as by what may be termed mere habit, did Sir John Appleby, lately the devoted pruner of his wife's roses, take charge of the mysterious affair at Drool Court.

And there, in the library, was indeed the Emir Hafrait, seated at the long table as Appleby had first glimpsed him. There was no sign of the man with the gun.

'Ah,' the Emir said. 'Here is our Professor at last, Mr Chitfield. Your other companion is unknown to me. However, you all have my permission to sit down.'

Appleby was the first to comply with this startling assumption of regality. He was also the first to speak.

'I regret to have to inform Your Excellency that a person garbed as you are garbed, and bearing a strong resemblance to yourself, has been brutally murdered in the grounds of this house.'

'Ah, indeed. But he will have his reward.'

'That is as it may be.' Appleby felt no temptation to enter into a theological discussion. 'But a stringent investigation alike of his presence here and of his death must be instituted at once. I must ask without more ado what you have to say about it – and about much else, I am inclined to believe.'

'May I inquire, sir, what right you have to address me in this peremptory fashion?' It was evident that the Emir Hafrait commanded excellent English.

'Certainly you may. I hold the Queen's warrant – and, as it happens, her commission as well. It is my duty to do what I can to preserve Her Majesty's peace.'

'You are, in fact, a magistrate?'

'Certainly I am a magistrate. And I am closely in touch with the Chief Constable of this district – who will, I hope, be joining us shortly. Meanwhile, it will greatly oblige me if Your Excellency will answer a few questions.'

'Very well.' The Emir inclined his head with dignity, and apparently by way of acknowledging this more accommodating manner of address.

'Basic to the situation I take it is the fact of your position being such that, wherever you go, there is always present some threat of a political nature to the safety of your person.'

'That is so. Professor McIlwraith could tell you about that.'

'Certainly I could.' McIlwraith now spoke for the first time. 'And about the difficulty over dress.'

'I think I have some understanding of that.' Appleby glanced at the Emir. 'I take it you are among those of your race or nation who will in no circumstances don Western clothes?'

'That is so. And I take strong exception, moreover, to Europeans donning the garments of my own countrymen. The spectacle of it has displeased me this afternoon.'

'No doubt,' McIlwraith said, 'Mr Chitfield arranged that there should be such persons with a purpose more sober than that of mere frolic.'

'Of course he did.' Appleby spoke with a touch of impatience. 'In fact he organized, in an amateur fashion and on a considerable scale, a state of affairs holding some affinity with the Emir's apparent habit of taking a kind of decoy around with him.'

'Just that,' Chitfield said. 'If there was to be an unobtrusive conference with the Emir, my fancy-dress party seemed just the thing to cover it. I made sure that there would be quite a number of sheiks around.'

'I would have discountenanced the idea had it been made clear to me.' The Emir spoke severely. 'I regard these masquerading people as an impertinence.'

'I don't quite see that,' Appleby said – feeling it rather hard that Mr Pring and his fellows should be thus aspersed. 'But, Mr Chitfield, you were certainly bringing innocent and unknowing people into hazard. The law might take a serious view of it. But that, for the moment, is by the by. The Emir is in considerable danger still. That's the situation to take account of at present.'

'Nevertheless I must say something further about the masquerade.' The Emir, as he made this announcement, was regarding his host with unconcealed disfavour. 'I was never before required to sit down beside circus clowns and Teddy bears. There was even, if I recollect aright, a Mickey Mouse.'

'Well, perhaps that was rather a mistake.' Chitfield said this in a tone of weak apology. 'It was simply that, at so early a stage in our negotiation, some of the fellows took the opportunity of not showing their hand.'

'Their faces, you mean,' the Emir said grimly. 'Although I thought it due to you as my host not to show my displeasure openly, I judged it an altogether unsuitable levity. I have, however, so far restrained my displeasure as to take a stroll through the absurd charade in progress here. I now propose to return to London.'

'Perhaps,' Appleby asked, 'taking the corpse of your unfortunate henchman with you?'

'Ah, that.' The Emir smiled faintly. 'Of course I much regret the man's death. But it is the custom in my family to have several such persons at one's disposal.'

'I fear, Your Excellency, that in this country it is a custom more honoured in the breach than the observance. Indeed, only diplomatic immunity may stand between you and considerable inconvenience. However, let us consider your return to London — which I myself regard as wholly desirable. How is it best to be accomplished without risk of some further fatality? The question can't be answered without rather more information than we have obtained so far. When, for example, was your meeting or conference or whatever it may have been called arranged to take place at Drool Court? Certain dispositions made by Mr Chitfield here suggest that it must have been some time ago.'

'Certainly — and it was about a fortnight ago.'

'Mr Chitfield then hit on the odd notion of tying it up with this fancy-dress affair. He persuaded a certain number of his friends to attend in the character of sheiks, with the notion that this would make your own presence less obtrusive. Incidentally, he positively forbade a young man who may be described as a family friend to assume such a character, which suggests his regarding mere business associates as curiously expendable. Mr Chitfield, you agree to that?'

'You can put it that way, I suppose. I certainly didn't want Cherry's boy to get mixed up in the affair.'

'So both you and the Emir may be said to have taken precautions. Yours included hiring a man with a gun, and his took the decidedly exotic form of bringing a spurious emir along with him. And now we must, I think, undertake a kind of census of sheiks. The task is complicated by the substantial possibility of several people turning up thus attired in a purely coincidental fashion. But let us assume that everybody now wandering around thus habited holds, as it were, a place in the story. Does Your Excellency suppose that any of your enemies, being bent on your assassination, would be likely to turn up — conceivably for religious reasons — in what I will venture to call their native costume?'

'Certainly not. They would clearly dress as unobtrusively as possible.'

'Quite so. But now we come to a curious fact. I happen to have become aware that three men, who apparently turned up here in ordinary dress, changed into Arab costume during the afternoon.'

'How on earth could they do that?' McIlwraith asked.

'Simply by hiring the stuff at the entrance to the fête. They had, one may suppose, tumbled to the existence of Mr Chitfield's pseudo-sheiks, and seen that by dressing up that way themselves they would place themselves within an essentially harmless group of persons. It would be quite a neat deception. The Emir, having heard about Mr Chitfield's dressing up of a number of his friends, would regard any person so dressed up as necessarily entirely harmless. He would not be on his guard if approached by one or more of them.' Appleby turned to the Emir. 'Your Excellency follows me?' he asked urbanely.

'Of course I follow you. But for how much longer am I to be constrained to do so?'

'Well, there are one or two further points. Those of the pseudo-sheiks who have the happiness of being our host's colleagues' – and Appleby glanced rather grimly at Mr Chitfield – 'are probably known to one another, and are likely to meet, converse, and perhaps stroll around in couples or groups. But you, Your Excellency, must be described as unique. There is only one of you at Drool, and not much observation would be required to pick you out were you walking through the place either accompanied by a European, such as the Professor here, or alone. This is a fact which may assist us later. Meantime, another inquiry occurs to me. We hear frequently enough of some shooting or bombing or other murderous achievement being claimed not merely as the action of a single group of terrorists but actually by two or more. It is like children at school, you know. The teacher asks, "Who threw that pellet?" and immediately two or three hands go proudly up in different corners of the room. Your Excellency will forgive the homeliness of the analogy. What I am concerned to know is whether there may be such rivals or competitors thirsting for your blood.'

'You phrase it a trifle crudely, perhaps. But it may well be so.' The Emir Hafrait paused for a moment. 'Might it be permissible to inquire at this rather late stage,' he asked, 'the more exact standing of the person by whom I am being addressed?'

'He is Sir John Appleby,' McIlwraith said – hastily, and as if here there had been a decided slip-up in protocol. 'Sir John may be described as having held, until his recent retirement, the position of highest authority in the English police force. Our system is difficult to describe with brevity. But that is more or less the fact of the matter.'

'Then let us proceed.' The Emir had bowed gravely, but scarcely with the air of a man notably impressed by what he had just heard. 'As for competitors – yes, indeed. I have enemies who are each other's enemies, too. Here again is something not to be described with brevity. But Sir John will be well acquainted with such situations. Amusing facts will filter through to him from your intelligence people, and from your Foreign Office. It is a state of affairs gossiped about in the clubs, is it not?' Achieving this stroke of sophistication appeared to put the Emir momentarily in good humour. 'Let us continue,' he said, 'this perhaps premature inquest over my corpse.'

'Competing groups of terrorists or activists or whatever they may call themselves,' Appleby said, 'may have different methods and different aims. One group may want a corpse, while another wants a hostage. And our own police, by collaring one group and locking them up or deporting them, may simply be clearing the field for another group to close in on its quarry. So we have to be a little careful, you will see. For example, I know nothing whatever about Your Excellency, except what you have told me yourself, and what Mr Chitfield here knows or believes he knows. For instance – and I hope you will not be offended at my offering it – that dead man may perfectly well be your own brother, and a little family feud have been taken one stage further by yourself this afternoon.'

'Dear me!' The Emir had merely raised his eyebrows. 'Your suggestion has at least ingenuity, although scarcely civility, to commend it.'

'And we must consider our own situation at the moment as a small group gathered in Mr Chitfield's library. From any evidence I have seen we may be in an entirely deserted house, lacking even the company of our host's friend with the gun. And outside is a congeries of fantastically garbed pleasure-seekers a quarter of a mile thick around us. There are also two policemen in plain clothes, and by this time perhaps several more in uniform as well. I am bound to say that I see a variety of undesirable possibilities, any one of which must be coped with as best we may. But ah! Here is the Chief Constable arrived to help us.'

XV

Colonel Pride had entered the library without knocking. Framed in the doorway, he stood silent for some moments, apparently viewing without much approval the room's owner and his two guests. He had abandoned his long-bow, but not his coat or even his hat of Lincoln green. It was the Emir who first spoke – and after glancing from Appleby to Pride and back again.

'Dear me!' he said. 'I do not recall seeing members of the English constabulary thus garbed before. No doubt it is full-dress uniform, and assumed in compliment to Mr Chitfield here – or even conceivably to myself.'

Colonel Pride, who was distinctly unprepared to be entertained by nonsense, took two steps into the room.

'Sir,' he said, 'I presume you to be the Emir Hafrait. And Sir John Appleby will no doubt have informed you that a man "garbed", as you would have it, precisely like yourself, and presumably a compatriot and perhaps retainer of your own, has met a violent death here not half an hour ago. His body was discovered in the deserted archery ground, transfixed by an arrow which had been discharged into his back. I can see no possibility of the fatality's having been any sort of accident. We are dealing with a crime, and one to be seen as only superficially bizarre. The assassin – to choose a term which may be faintly less disagreeable to you than "murderer" – may well have had a firearm in his pocket. But he seized an opportunity of going silently to work. And, of course, necessarily from behind. A close scrutiny from the front might have told him he had the wrong man.'

'My dear Chief Constable, sad as it must seem, I am by

no means astounded. Attempts upon my life, or at the seizing of my person, are at present quite the order of the day. And I take such precautions as I can.'

'That, sir, is precisely what I intend to do myself. I have sent for a suitable conveyance – it may be called of the armour-plated sort – to convey you back to London and to your Embassy, or whatever it may be. It will be here within half an hour. Meanwhile, if you have any information to give, I am prepared to receive it.'

Appleby, although he had listened to this speech with considerable satisfaction, found it necessary to intervene.

'I certainly agree,' he said, 'that Drool Court and its owner will be well advised to dispense with His Excellency's company as briskly as may be. Indeed, I don't much like the sound of that half-hour. The murderer and his confederates – for the minimum number of them is three – will certainly know by now that they got the wrong man. And we have to face the fact that we are in an uncommonly vulnerable situation. I know, Tommy, that you may have something in your own pocket. But here we are, in this oddly depopulated mansion, and in a ground-floor room with a door and four windows. A suitable kind of bomb, pitched through any of these apertures, could despatch all five of us in an instant. And I gather that your own couple of men are unarmed – not to speak of their being pretty well lost in the crowd. So there's absolutely no possibility of quickly throwing any sort of cordon round this uncommonly large house.'

'In half an hour, yes; immediately, no.' Colonel Pride paused for a moment on this. 'So just what had we better do?'

'One thing you shall *not* do.' It was the Emir who took up the Colonel's question. 'And that is to persuade me to leave this house other than in my own motor car.'

'Which is now in the temporary car park?' Appleby asked.

'Certainly it is.'

'And with a chauffeur waiting in it?'

'Unhappily not. It was the man they have killed who drove me down. But I can very well drive it myself – and in the circumstances I consider that to be the suitable thing. I always carry a key with me.'

'In that case, and as you appear to regard the Chief Constable's suggestion as demeaning, your own car it will have to be – and as quickly as possible.'

'We'll send a fellow down with your key,' Colonel Pride said, 'and he will bring the car up to the house at once. CD, no doubt; and with a little flag on it as well. It shouldn't be hard to spot.'

'Just so, Tommy. And spotting is precisely what we don't want. The Emir must make his way to his car, and not the other way round. Mohammed must go to the mountain, in fact.' Appleby paused, glanced at the Emir, and saw that this little quip had been received with extreme disfavour. 'I beg your pardon,' he said. 'But I hope you take my point. You must be got to your car – and invisibly, so to speak, if it can be managed. Would you consent to quit this house as Robin Hood? I hasten to add that, according to one school of thought, he is believed to have been a great English nobleman. It would leave either the Chief Constable or myself a little bare to the winds for a time. But that would scarcely signify.'

'Certainly not.' The Emir spoke with decided hauteur. 'I regard your suggestion as wholly unacceptable.'

'In that case you must go exactly as you are. But – only for a couple of minutes – you must excuse me.' As he said this, Appleby turned round, strode rapidly across the library, and disappeared through the door by which he had entered it. The three gentlemen thus abruptly abandoned had scarcely time to recover from their surprise at this odd behaviour before Appleby was back with them again. For Appleby it certainly was, although he was now fully attired in Arab costume, and regarding them through outsize dark glasses.

'I hope,' he asked, 'that I don't look too convincing?'

'I can't say that you do, John.' Colonel Pride appeared to feel that the occasion required candour. 'But, even so, how the dickens —'

'A not unengaging young man called Tibby Fancroft abandoned this rig-out in the corridor before proposing to present himself to Mr Chitfield for the purpose of making him an apology. The things seem to fit me not too badly. But I have to look unconvincing, all the same. Let me explain.'

'Perhaps you, too, ought to apologize,' the Emir said icily. The taking of liberties with his national costume seemed to be invariably a sore point with him.

'It's like this,' Appleby said briskly. 'The would-be assassins became aware quite early in the afternoon that Mr Chitfield's pseudo-sheiks — as I've ventured to call them — were in abundant supply. And they concluded, quite correctly, that they had been persuaded to dress themselves up in this way simply to confuse matters. Moreover they took it for granted — and quite erroneously — that the Emir himself was privy to what was going on. So three of them — and we must always bear in mind that there may be more — hired three Arab costumes, which they are no doubt still wearing now. In this way they thought to make themselves seem particularly harmless. They were adding themselves to the number of those whom the Emir, and anybody concerned for the Emir's safety, would be entirely off their guard about. And now here is the crucial point. The unfortunate man whom the Emir brought to Drool Court with him having been murdered, the Emir is left, we may say, *sui generis*. And the last thing he is likely to do is to attach himself to, and converse with, any pseudo-sheik about the place. They are now looking out for an Emir who is decidedly a loner. Which is why he and I are now going to take a ramble together down to the car park. It is also why I hope that I myself look patently bogus. And if Your Excellency will consent to looking a little bogus yourself — shambling along, say, in a distinctly unimpressive manner — I have little doubt that we shall reach your car without anything undesirable happening to us.'

It might have been expected that this extraordinary speech would be followed by silence, at least for an appreciable space. But what did follow was more extraordinary still. The Emir Hafrait was amused. He was even condescending to laugh. Richard Chitfield, clearly alarmed by something wholly outside his experience of his haughty and severely mannered guest, gaped rather as if there were suddenly being revealed to him some natural monstrosity such as a two-headed calf. Colonel Pride was merely looking thoughtful and dubious, perhaps estimating how the proposed prank would stand up, if anything untoward happened, before a judge of the High Court.

'A prince,' the Emir said, 'pretending to be a plebeian pretending to be a prince. It is a fitting end to the very great piece of nonsense perpetrated here this afternoon. Sir John, I am with you. Let us go.'

At this moment, however, there came a knock on the library door.

In fact there came three knocks – the second by no means hurrying after the first, nor the third after the second. The effect was curiously ominous. Colonel Pride's hand moved towards Robin Hood's pocket. Sir John Appleby momentarily indulged the thought that if Fate had the habit of knocking on people's doors other than in a merely metaphorical way this would be just the manner of it. Then the door opened and a tall figure robed in white stood revealed. The tall figure took two solemn paces forward and then raised a solemn arm in air.

'Grace to Maleldil,' the intruder said in a deep voice.

'And who the devil are you?' It was with some difficulty that Mr Chitfield, already somewhat overwrought by the recent turn of events, managed to produce this brusque challenge.

'Grace to Maleldil,' the mysterious visitant reiterated in a yet deeper tone.

'Grace to Maleldil,' Appleby said. It was clear to him that here was one of the Basingstoke Druids – perhaps, indeed, the Archdruid, if a hierarchical system existed among them. And he recalled the Order of the Golden Dawn. Certainly the Basingstoke Druids borrowed whatever took their fancy. This peculiar salutation came, he happened to know, from a rather high-toned work of space fiction. But echoing it produced an immediate emollient effect.

'Well, this is it,' the druid said on a relaxed and colloquial note. 'Everybody has to be out of the house in twenty minutes. That's for the Perlustration. It's only in an empty house that we can do the Perlustration – particularly when it's with the Asperges. The Asperges don't work, they don't, with outsiders around.'

'Go away. Go away at once.' Mr Chitfield did his best to assume a commanding manner. 'We have serious matters to discuss here, and want none of your nonsense. So clear out.'

'It's your missus we have our contract with.' The druid's tone had changed yet again, and verged upon the truculent. '"See there's nobody left in the house," she said. And that's why I'm speaking to you now.'

'Oh, very well.' Mr Chitfield spoke resignedly. It was evident that in domestic matters – and this was in an odd fashion domestic – he was habituated to letting his wife have her way. 'But I understood there was to be an audience for your event.'

'That's outside. Chairs and benches are being arranged there now. It's the candles and torches and the like showing through the windows that your crowd will see. And then the procession to our vehicle. With the Grand Chant, that will be. We've made it clear, you know, that the Grand Chant's another extra.'

'No doubt – and you're welcome to your imbecile extras. But go away now, and leave us to our affairs.'

'Grace to Maleldil,' the druid said — and retired with dignity from the library.

'And now we'll get going,' Appleby said briskly. 'But, Tommy, just how is it with this extraordinary fête? Have you simply let it go ahead, despite what has happened to the Emir's unfortunate follower?'

'Yes.' The Chief Constable nodded emphatically. 'It's known there's been some sort of accident on that archery field. But I've given instruction that what's actually happened shouldn't get spread around. If there's diplomatic dynamite lurking in the affair it's probably wise to keep a low profile until we get a word from the FO.'

'I suppose you're right there. And, in any case, a big crowd still milling around is to our advantage for the moment. But the most ticklish part of our plan comes first. Getting out of the house, that is. If one of the villains saw the two of us emerging through the front door, he'd be pretty thick if he didn't turn suspicious straight away.'

'Then we must emerge from the back, and by way of the servants' quarters.' This came, rather surprisingly, from the Emir. It was evident that something in the spirit of the impending exploit appealed to him. 'Mr Chitfield can no doubt guide us to the appropriate corner of his modest country retreat.'

Mr Chitfield, although this description of Drool Court could scarcely have been agreeable to him, concurred in the proposal at once. He had plainly had enough of his exalted guest, however valuable a business prospect he might be. Between sheiks and druids, he might have been feeling, there was just nothing to choose.

'John,' Colonel Pride said abruptly, 'you'd better take this little affair along with you. It can't be called at all an impressive weapon, but it may be better than nothing.' As he spoke, Colonel Pride produced a decidedly small automatic pistol.

'No, Tommy, I think not.' Appleby had shaken his head decisively. 'This whole affair is so uncommonly ramifying and obscure that you may turn out to be in more need of it than I am. But it puts another question in my head.' Appleby turned to Chitfield. 'What about that guard of yours with the gun?' he asked. 'He might turn out useful, after all.'

'When the meeting was over I told him to clear out. It struck me he'd been a mistake. When he got up and pointed the damned thing at Tibby Fancroft and yourself I didn't care for it at all. So I told him to make himself scarce and send in his bill.'

'It was an entirely prudent decision,' the Chief Constable said severely. 'No good ever comes of having thick-skulled thugs hanging around with illegal weapons. As things have turned out, I'll admit that we might have found some use for him. But if he has taken his departure, we'd better not hear of him again.'

'And I thought, you see, that the Emir would be going back to London at once.' Richard Chitfield offered this further explanation in an aggrieved tone, as if the Emir's continued enjoyment of his hospitality had been distinctly bad form.

'Well,' Appleby said, 'he's going back now – and the sooner I see his car departing down the drive the happier I'll be. So be so good, Mr Chitfield, to get us out of this house and into that crowd as unobtrusively as you can.'

'It had better not be by the kitchens, but through the conservatory and the string of glass-houses beyond it. They're so crammed with damned-fool plants that nobody can see you going through, and at the other end there's only the old stable yard. When you're through that you'll come out bang in the middle of things.'

And thus revealing himself as far from an ardent horticulturist, Mr Richard Chitfield led the way out of his library.

XVI

The conservatory at Drool Court proved to be a large and lofty affair, outrageously out of keeping with the character of the house itself. At its centre rose a species of lantern or cupola, the greater part of which was occupied by the head of a palm tree that somehow suggested itself as having given up a vain struggle to escape from the place and to have relapsed into a sulky lassitude. The Emir Hafrait paused before it, and his features briefly underwent a change which might have signalled either amusement or commiseration – or conceivably a mingling of the two. But when he then turned his glance upon Appleby it was in a fashion that was entirely serious.

'It is a question, Sir John,' he said, 'whether I ought to have placed myself under your conduct in this way. You live, I presume, in retirement?'

'Certainly I do.'

'But you feel what may be termed the common citizen's obligation to guard, as you have expressed it, your Sovereign's peace?'

'I suppose it's just that. Shall we move on?'

'Not, if you please, for one moment. I must explain to you that the measure of our common danger is greater than you perhaps imagine. That I was to be here at the person Chitfield's house today appears to have been "leaked", as they say, to a highly undesirable extent. So you are not to suppose that what threatens is confined to three men absurdly disguised as belonging to Chitfield's impertinent bunch of pseudo-sheiks. I appreciate, may I say, your wit in so naming them.'

'I am obliged to Your Excellency.'

'There may be as many as a dozen men, by no means necessarily well disposed the one to another, who are here with the intention of killing me. A dozen assassins, Sir John, or "hit-men" as now appears to be the common phrase. That I have survived up to this moment in what may perfectly fairly be called a trap, is due merely to the fact that they one and all are ignobly anxious to kill without being found out. But now consider what you and I are doing. We are making our way back to the easily identified motor car in which I came to Drool. Is it not only too likely that a skilled sharpshooter has his sights trained upon it at this moment?'

'I can't say that the possibility has eluded me. Mind the step.' Appleby had contrived to get this loquacious potentate into motion again, and they were passing from the main conservatory to a string of interconnected greenhouses. 'I must explain to you that Colonel Pride, the Chief Constable, is an old friend of mine and a yet older friend of my wife; that he has been for some wholly obscure reason inadequately briefed about your situation; and that I am simply making it my business to lend a hand in getting you back to town. Ah! Here we are in open air again, and presumably in what Chitfield called the old stable yard. And nothing stabled in it except that Range Rover. Oddly enough, it is familiar to me. When found, make a note of.'

'I beg your pardon?' The Emir, being presumably unfamiliar with *Dombey and Son*, was naturally perplexed.

'I know its owner – although only to the extent of having exchanged a few words with him – and it is just possible he may be of help to us. But why he has driven in here, I can't tell. His business is collecting snakes.'

'Snakes?' The Emir was yet more perplexed. 'Serpents?'

'Yes, indeed. They do happen in England, although there is seldom much mischief in them. The man is simply making a collection for scientific purposes in a laboratory attached to the University of Oxford. But now let us go ahead – through the crowd and down to the car park. And let me remind Your Excellency to shuffle. If you can contrive once or twice to trip over your robe, so much the better.'

This time the Emir Hafrait seemed undecided whether to smile or frown. He was, no doubt, unaccustomed to being even gently made fun of. But he moved on at once, and when he next spoke it was not in displeasure. 'My dear Sir John, I really don't like this at all – although the idea did amuse me when you advanced it. With one of my own people it would be another matter. They have their code, and we understand one another. But to lead into danger a person of eminence in the country of which I am a guest – that, I do not care for at all. It is itself a kind of shuffling, as you call it. I would be better pleased to go on alone.'

'Leaving me ashamed of myself? My word went with my suggestion, and I'd be breaking it if I left off now.'

'An unanswerable argument, Sir John. And I might do worse than quit this curious affair we call life in the company of an English gentleman. It occurs to me that we have not shaken hands. May we do so now?'

So the Emir Hafrait and Sir John Appleby solemnly performed this ritual act before stepping once more into the hubbub of Mr Richard Chitfield's hypertrophied garden party.

XVII

Surveying the scene Appleby received the impression that the entire ramshackle occasion had turned out to be a fair success. This ran very much contrary to his earlier expectations. The diversity of the amusements on offer, together with the fact that the wearing of fancy dress becomes somewhat irksome and even embarrassing if sustained for long, would have resulted – so he had thought – in a very general inclination to feel that one had enjoyed one's money's worth and might now go home. But there was certainly no drift towards the car park – which was sited just within such a real park as Drool Court possessed, with beyond it the fringes of that extensive area of woodland in which Appleby had encountered Richard Chitfield's disconsolate younger daughter the day before. The military band on the terrace was concealed behind a corner of the mansion, but its unwearied strains – still muted in deference to Mr Chitfield's theatrical enterprise nearly a quarter of a mile away – continued to provide such entertainment as one cared to listen to.

Equally unwearied appeared to be the *passeggiata* performed by a large number of the variously disguised guests, so that the effect of a huge and mobile flowerbed was still unimpaired. The only sheik – pseudo or otherwise – at present on view was the previously parched Mr Pring. He was conversing, clearly in a deferential manner, with Nick Bottom, the textile tycoon. Nick had so far relaxed as to take off his ass's head, but not to part with it; he was carrying it under one arm in a manner suggesting a monster which had miraculously survived decollation and was on the way to have the surprising achievement commemorated in the studio of some painter who went in for that sort of thing. In the middle distance the hot-air balloon, which now appeared to be straining at its moorings, happened to present itself behind these two conversing persons, and thus afforded the suggestion of a bright cloud or nimbus entirely appropriate to such a supernatural occasion.

'We have a couple of hundred yards to cover,' Appleby said to the Emir. 'The first hundred, as you can see, is more or less within the fringes of the crowd. After that, we shall be noticeably on our own. The car park appears deserted, and at the moment nobody else is making for it.'

'But do I not see a police car at the far end of the ground?' The Emir Hafrait was thoroughly alert. 'What is called a Panda car, I believe. And there appears to be an officer in it.'

'Perfectly true – and he is in some sort of radio communication with the outer world. But he won't be armed, and I don't think we should improve matters by making our way to him. Incidentally, since the car park is at a distinctly lower level than we are, we have a better view of it as a whole than he has. But what about your own car – can you point it out to me?' Appleby paused for a moment. 'But not, Your Excellency, too ostentatiously. Remember that we are two pseudo-sheiks, simply wandering around. Perhaps we are interested in motor cars, and are therefore taking an idle stroll in their direction. But just a stroll it must continue to be. It wouldn't do at all to stride purposefully ahead.'

'Quite so. And my own car is the grey Rolls-Royce almost in the middle of the park. You can perhaps distinguish, Sir John, what Colonel Pride was pleased to describe as its little flag.'

'I certainly can.' It was evident to Appleby that national flags were among the things that the Emir was inclined to be touchy about. 'I suppose,' he asked abruptly, 'that the doors are sure to be locked?'

'The doors of my car? I suppose so, too. Yet it is only a supposition. I did not myself see, that is to say, that my unfortunate compatriot performed the action.'

'But you yourself have a key to the doors as well as to the ignition?'

'Most certainly.' The Emir, while doing his best to move forward in a slouching and plebeian fashion, frowned majestically. 'Has it occurred to you, Sir John, that the nearer two fancy-dress sheiks approach to an authentic sheik's car the more likely is the enemy, if watching from some point of vantage, to penetrate to the true state of the case?'

'Indeed it has.' Appleby frowned in his turn. The two men were now clear of the crowd – which at least obviated the necessity of maintaining their features in a state of contented vacancy. 'It will be our plan abruptly to change gear, as it were, at the crisis of the operation. We shall have paused beside one car and another in a con- noisseur's fashion. But when we get to your Rolls, you will unlock the door in a flash, jump in, start the engine, and depart from Drool Court with all the formidable acceleration that such a vehicle commands.'

'And you, too, Sir John?'

'Dear me, no. Nobody is going to risk capture for the satisfaction of taking a pot-shot at a retired policeman. And there are one or two other matters at Drool that I am not without curiosity about. So I shall wave you farewell, and return to see what's what. But here we are. Let us make our first pause before that sporty little Morgan.'

This they did – and went through the same pantomime two or three times more. It was at least an activity that no one who knew the Emir Hafrait would suppose it likely he would indulge in. And then the moment had come. The Rolls was before them.

'Unlocked.' The Emir's hand had gone out to the door beside the driver's seat. 'So now –'

'*Stop!*' It was perhaps seldom that Sir John Appleby had put more urgency into this injunction. 'And stroll on.'

It was equally seldom, perhaps, that the Emir Hafrait had for many years obeyed a command. But he did so now. And he glanced almost mildly at Appleby.

'You have changed your mind?' he asked.

'Yes, I have. That the car has been left unlocked and therefore accessible changes the whole state of the case. Somebody may have slipped into it totally unobserved, and left a small token of his intrusion behind him. And I've been an idiot not to think of it. Your having turned the key on the ignition might have activated something more than the engine.'

'How very true.' The Emir remained entirely calm. 'What is called – or used to be called – an infernal machine. My dear Sir John, we must think again.'

'Certainly we must. And you, on your part, if I may say so, must rethink that disinclination to depart only in a dignified fashion in your own vehicle. We will stroll on to that Panda car, and the constable must instantly drive you away in it. I am fairly well known in these parts, and he is unlikely to resist my authority for a moment. You agree?'

'I do.' The Emir Hafrait accompanied this reply with a grave inclination of the head certainly not commanded by any sheik of the Pring order.

For some moments the two men walked on in silence, and then the police car came fully into view.

'Yes,' the Emir said. 'Yes – we are distinctly out of luck, are we not?'

'We are, indeed.' Appleby glanced only briefly at the Panda car, which was now deserted. 'The fellow has been called away again – I suppose on his walkie-talkie. And he certainly won't have left *his* car un-locked. It's an absolute instruction with them to make all secure even if they're away for no more than five minutes.'

'May he perhaps have received, from a police station or some such place, a message which he is now conveying to Colonel Pride in Chitfield's house?'

'That may well be it. And I think our best course may be to return to the house ourselves.'

'And join, Sir John, in what I think I heard called the Perlustration?'

'That's still a little time ahead. But I can't say I altogether like the look of the Basingstoke Druids – and how Chitfield's wife came by their services I don't know at all. Let us take a glance, Your Excellency, at another car or two, and then retrace our steps.'

'I am under your command, Sir John.' The Emir said this distinctly in his more majestic manner, while at the same time remembering to toddle forward in a Pring-like fashion. 'I am full of admiration,' he continued, 'for the English police. Nothing ruffles them – and any outbreak of armed violence appears to be the last thing that comes into their heads.'

'Just so.' Appleby was amused by this obliquely phrased criticism. 'And they like, as you heard Pride expressing it, to keep a low profile as they work. From the start of things today, Pride has had a couple of his men in plain clothes keeping their eyes open amid this confusing jamboree. But they are certainly not armed. And now he has sent for reinforcements – which probably means a dozen uniformed men, with perhaps a couple of reliably cool-headed marksmen among them. As a last resort, of course, there are the Armed Forces of the Crown.'

'Which could be sent in, I suppose, only on the authority of the Prime Minister?'

'Ah, that, Your Excellency, is rather a deep matter. I am inclined to think that the Lord Lieutenant of the county, or even perhaps at a pinch the High Sheriff, could set the troops marching.'

This badinage, which the Emir Hafrait appeared to accept as an agreeable novelty, brought the two men back into the old stable yard. The Range Rover was still here. But now the Range Rover's owner was there as well.

*

It seemed civil to pass the time of day with this itinerant herpetologist, and Appleby did so.

'Good afternoon,' he said. 'I hope you have enjoyed good hunting.'

'Good afternoon. Yes, indeed. But dear me!' For a second the herpetologist seemed at a loss before this remark from a stranger strangely attired. Then the explanation came to him. 'We exchanged – did we not, sir? – a few words yesterday afternoon. My name is Gillam. This appears to be a very large-scale fancy-dress affair. And I take it that you and your friend decided to impersonate the same sort of person.'

'My name is Appleby. And that is not quite the situation. What you say holds good, after a fashion, of myself – but my companion must be described as in his ordinary clothes. So let me, in fact, present you to the Emir Hafrait.'

'How do you do?' It didn't appear that Mr Gillam was much struck by the oddity of this situation, nor by the fact that the Emir had made him a very formal bow. But he did appear to feel that he should explain his own presence. 'I've been doing a good deal of my collecting,' he said, 'on Mr Chitfield's land. But he and I haven't met, since I received his permission to go ahead simply by an exchange of letters. So I thought a polite call might be in order before I returned to Oxford. I drove in here intending to walk up to the house and present myself. But when I saw this tremendous carnival affair going forward I decided I'd be merely a nuisance, and that another letter would be the polite thing. Would you be inclined to agree with me?'

'On the whole, yes.' Appleby had removed his dark glasses, and it was evident that he was mildly amused by this appeal. 'Mr Chitfield may be described this afternoon as having a good deal on his hands. It's all in the interest of some charity or other.' Appleby glanced at the Emir. 'Or nearly all.'

'Well, at least I've contributed. They made me buy a

ticket at the main gate. And I steered myself in here because snakes, you know, don't care for a hubbub. It unsettles them. They're sensitive creatures.'

'That's most interesting.' Appleby was reflecting that the Emir, too, was in his way a sensitive creature – and wondering whether, this being so, he could be persuaded to take a ride along with a van-load of grass snakes and adders. And, while he was thus reflecting, Mr Gillam (or Dr Gillam, or Professor Gillam) found something more to say.

'Then I'll be on my way – going back as I came. There seems to be only one carriage drive to this fellow Chitfield's place. From what I've heard of him, I'd have expected him to go in for something of more consequence, so to speak. And it's odd that there should actually be chaps who have chosen this afternoon to dig a hole in the middle of it. Some emergency with the water or electricity, I imagine. Quite a small hole, and one of the fellows waved me past it. But do you know? As I've paid my penny, I might as well have a look round the show before driving off.'

'Not a bad idea,' Appleby said. 'The Relief of Mafeking must be due any time now. It's one of the highlights, and you'll be guided to it by the shindy.'

'Most amusing. Boy Scouts and their kidney putting on a turn, I suppose. But I'll just batten things down first.' And Gillam gestured towards the Range Rover. 'Awkward if some of these little chaps got going among the crowd.'

'Particularly among the ladies,' the Emir said unexpectedly. 'Women are sometimes terrified of serpents to a quite irrational degree. But at least at Oxford you have no women to be perturbed by them.'

With this startling leap a century backwards, the usually well-informed Emir Hafrait offered the herpetologist a courteously dismissive bow, and walked on with Appleby through the greenhouses.

XVIII

In the main conservatory, beneath the lofty palm tree's shade, Appleby and the Emir found themselves confronted by Colonel Pride. The Chief Constable was now accompanied by a uniformed policeman – presumably the office who had been in charge of the Panda car and in direct radio contact with the advancing forces of law and order now on their way to Drool Court. The constable (like all such subordinate characters in mystery stories) might have been described as stolid. Colonel Pride, on the other hand, betrayed a certain irritation – an irritation, indeed, that shaded into something like animosity as his glance travelled from Appleby to the Emir.

'What the devil has gone wrong?' he demanded. 'Has somebody made off with the fellow's – with the Emir's – blasted Rolls-Royce?'

'Not quite that, Tommy. But it was unlocked as well as unattended, and probably under nobody's observation for half an hour at a time. So there is just a possibility that it has been booby-trapped.'

'Then why didn't you shove him into your own car?' The Chief Constable seemed unaware of anything discourteous in this manner of expressing himself. But the Emir, if offended, evinced no sign of displeasure. He might have been thinking of something totally other than his present situation. 'Did he jib at it?'

'He well might have done. But the car happens to be Judith's baby Fiat, the *topolino*. You couldn't hide a hen in it, let alone an eagle. And, as it happens, I've come across evidence that the booby-trap idea is being put into operation elsewhere. Bang under the drive to this house.

The fact has been unconsciously vouched for by an eminent Oxford herpetologist.'

'A *what*? Well, never mind. What do we do next?'

'Obviate the risk of something merely bloody-minded. Not much of a risk, but we needn't take chances. Your reinforcements are on the way to Drool now?'

'Of course they are. Several cars packed with them.'

'Stop them at once.' Appleby – not very properly – turned to the constable. 'You can do that?'

'Yes, sir.' The constable tapped the small radio contraption hanging on his chest. 'Just what am I to say?'

'They are to stop instantly, parking their cars on the roadside. An adequate number of them must block traffic at either end of the drive until they have made a careful examination of its surface and satisfied themselves that it has not been mined or booby-trapped. The remaining officers are to make their way here on foot through the wood and the park.'

'Very good, sir.' The constable glanced cautiously at his official superior officer and received a brisk confirmatory nod.

'Perhaps I may be permitted to offer a comment?' The Emir Hafrait made this inquiry in a suitably ironic tone. 'I am not surprised at the scale on which this murderous operation is developing. First my car, and then, for good measure, the drive along which I may pass in it, or in another vehicle. But I do not think that my adversaries would blow up a large number of policemen on the side. They have a better sense than that of what is relevant. And now do we go back to the good Chitfield's house, and to the further company of our friend the Professor?'

'It will no doubt be best that Your Excellency and Colonel Pride should do just that,' Appleby said. 'I myself want to take a further short stroll through the fête.'

'Why the deuce should you do that, John?' The Chief Constable appeared almost alarmed. 'Best to keep together, I'd say.'

'I'll join you – and, I suppose, the druids – almost

immediately. I'm rather interested in the Basingstoke Druids. But I have just a small spot of what you might call contingency planning to get through first.' And with this Appleby gave a casual nod, and walked away.

'Odd chap,' Colonel Pride said. 'But devilish deep at times. I've relied on him quite surprisingly every now and then. Very acute – very acute indeed – is Appleby. And after all those years pretty well doing standard leather-bottom stuff behind a desk in New Scotland Yard. Remarkable thing.'

'Your commendation, my dear Colonel, does not surprise me. I have myself considerable confidence in your colleague. I wonder whether – since he seems to have retired from his important English command – he would consider an appointment overseas?'

'I don't know at all, I'm sure.' And Colonel Pride glanced in mild astonishment at one whom he felt decidedly to be an unwelcome guest. 'Worth asking him, I suppose. He has a wife with a nice little property and isn't in need of money. But no harm in having a go.'

The Chief Constable felt that he had dealt with this bizarre inquiry rather well. The thought of John Appleby beefing up one set of ruffians against another in some outlandish corner of the globe entertained him very much. But now he made a polite gesture towards the house, and they both returned to the somewhat precarious shelter of its library.

Appleby, as a solitary perambulating sheik, found himself not liking things at all. It wasn't that he lacked a fairly distinct view of what had to be done. By one means or another, the Emir Hafrait must be whisked clear of Drool Court and all its present absurdities as rapidly as possible. But there was something rambling and untidy about the entire situation, a lack of anything that could be called a clear-cut mystery at the centre of it, which was decidedly not to his taste. It was true that some minor puzzles still cluttered up the main action. Where, for example, did the Basingstoke Druids fit in – if indeed they fitted in at all? Were they to be reckoned among the enemy in any significant regard? There was undoubtedly something bogus about them, which could escape the observation only of somebody as woolly-minded as Mrs Chitfield, their sponsor at Drool. If they were in any way an element in the operation designed to kill or kidnap Hafrait, then that operation at least commanded hugger-mugger or miching mallecho on a lavish scale.

As Appleby reflected on this he became aware that preparations were going forward for the druids' final turn: the solemn Perlustration of Drool Court. Two rows of chairs had been arranged in a semicircle before the house for those of Mr Chitfield's guests who cared to sit rather than stand through the ceremony, and beyond this there was a species of roped-off lane at the further end of which was now parked an entirely prosaic motor-coach in which the celebrants were presumably to return to Basingstoke. Appleby recalled that the dwelling had to be entirely vacated before the rites began, and he wondered whether, in the peculiar circumstances obtaining, Mr Chitfield would put his foot down so far as this aspect of the nonsense went. At the moment Chitfield, McIlwraith and the Emir were presumably within the precarious refuge of the library. Appleby felt he had better get back to them as quickly as was compatible with the business he now had in hand. So, for a start, he lost no time in searching out his recent acquaintance the Oxford herpe-tologist.

'Yes – yes, indeed,' the herpetologist said. 'I appreciate the situation, and have little doubt that what you suggest would have the desired effect. But I am bound to say that I feel most reluctant to agree to your request. It would be a most awkward yarn with which to return to Oxford. No, really – I think you must hold me excused, Mr – Dear me! I'm afraid I didn't catch your name.'

'Appleby. John Appleby.'

'Great God in heaven!' The herpetologist (whose own name we know to be Gillam) produced this profane ejaculation with sudden extraordinary energy. 'Sir John Appleby! My dear sir, your name is a legend among us. In the senior common room of my college, that is; and it may well be with the undergraduates as well. The celebrated affair was long before my time, but you may be sure I have heard of it in considerable detail. The manner, that is, of your solving the mystery of our then President's having been murdered in his Lodging. Yes, indeed – the unfortunate Josiah Umpleby. Of course I never set eyes on him. It must have been many years ago.'

'1936, Dr Gillam.'

'Dear me! Is that so? If it had been 1066 I think we should still be talking about it. And now my services are wholly at your disposal, I need hardly say.'

Such may be the uses – Appleby reflected as he made for his next objective – of even minor celebrity. And now fortune again favoured him. Scattered on the grass before Mr Chitfield's theatre were about a dozen boys who could be seen at a glance as not at all pleased with things. They were clothed, somewhat anachronistically, in combat-jackets, and stacked beside them in orthodox threesomes were the service rifles which had presumably held at bay the Boer forces intent upon capturing that legendary township in Bechuanaland. Only Master William Birch-Blackie, alias Colonel Baden-Powell, was on his feet, and he was employing them in a kind of gloomy sentry-go in front of his companions.

'Well, William,' Appleby said in what he hoped was a breezy fashion, 'did everything turn out as it should? Mafeking was relieved in the nick of time?'

'Yes, it was. And no it didn't.' The hero of the Boer War had last seen his father's elderly friend dressed up as Robin Hood, and had thought this stupid enough. That the old chap should now have taken it into his head to assume the appearance of a camel-driver or some such was really a bit on the pitiful side. William was still much disenchanted with the whole afternoon, as his next remarks showed. 'The siege business was as tame as you wouldn't believe. It might have been a silly game at a kids' party. Not a shot was fired. We're all pretty chuffed, Sir John. I can tell you that.'

'I'm sorry to hear it. No ammo on issue?'

'Of course we were given ammo. Two clips of blank to each of us. But then Mr Chitfield sent a message that there mustn't be any firing because it might alarm the ladies.'

'What about those bayonets, William?'

'Oh, we fixed bayonets, all right – and did a charge with them. We know all about it, of course, since we've all done our first year in the CCF at school. And a fixed bayonet is a damn sight more dangerous than a blank cartridge, believe you me.'

'Most certainly it is.' And Appleby nodded sagely. 'As a matter of fact, I have something rather less tame to suggest to you.'

'Just to me, or to the whole platoon?'

'To the whole lot of you, certainly. And it's a genuine para-military operation I have in mind.'

What this produced from Master William Birch-Blackie was a long appraising stare. But when he turned away it was to give a word of command.

'All you chaps,' he shouted, 'gather round! On your feet! Jump to it, I say! One two, one two!'

And so, in next to no time at all, Sir John Appleby was uttering wonderful and astounding words. The recently enacted siege of Mafeking had been a make-believe siege and had no doubt been extremely boring for everyone concerned. But it had been a make-believe siege within a perfectly real siege. He wouldn't go into much detail, since time was pressing. In outline the situation was this: somebody rather important (important enough, Appleby contrived to suggest in passing, to enjoy the services of a retired Commissioner of Metropolitan Police) was enduring virtually siege conditions at Drool Court now. It had to be made possible for him to break out, and there was a role that William Birch-Blackie and his thoroughly soldierlike companions could play. Appleby said only a little more than this, and when he had finished William had only a single brief question to ask.

'When you blow a whistle, sir?'

'Just that. I'll borrow one from a bobby – and know how to blow it, because I was once a bobby myself.'

'Sir!'

'Always remember' – Appleby said solemnly and to his auditory at large – 'that every private soldier carries a Field-Marshal's baton in his knapsack.'

Apart from these rapidly recruited *soldats d'élite*, Richard Chitfield's theatre and its surroundings were now deserted. The hot-air balloon, although inflated to the point at which it had assumed the proportions of an up-ended pear, was still at its moorings, and only a small clump of people were any longer paying any attention to it. Interest appeared now centred on Drool Court itself. Surveying the scene from what was still a respectful distance, Appleby could distinguish that all the seats ranged in front of the house were occupied, and that a considerable crowd of Mr Chitfield's visitors were standing behind them. It was evident that only in the Perlustration did any great interest remain at this oddly contrived fête. And this, Appleby thought, was just as it should be. The crowd, having waited thus far in expectation of an out-of-the-way spectacle, were now unlikely to call it a day and make for home before this expectation had been gratified. So the policemen still probably treating the drive as a prohibited area would not be having too ticklish a time of it. And a little congestion round Drool Court itself would be just right for what he had in mind.

And now – wasting no time, yet preserving something of the purposelessness proper in a pseudo-sheik –

Appleby made his way to the balloon. When he arrived at it he was at once confirmed in the impression that it had – at least in a metaphorical sense – misfired. Perhaps it had failed, for some technical reason, to take off at its advertised time, so that all but a few gazers had drifted away. Its aeronaut, previously glimpsed as habited in a fashion designed for the exploration of outer space, had divested himself of these somewhat theatrical properties, and was lounging against the basket-like contraption in which he should by now, it was to be supposed, have been wafted many leagues from Drool. He was a small dark man, who somehow immediately suggested himself as of a socially unassuming order. He also suggested, at least to a retired policeman, a degree of inebriety which might have brought him within the scope of the law had his vehicle been designed to perform on terra firma rather than in the heavens. Undue delay, perhaps, had led to his making too many short walks to Mr Chitfield's bar.

This was a slightly discouraging state of affairs. A drunk some thousands of feet in air is probably quite as dangerous as a drunk on the A4. On the other hand, he might with luck be the more ready to accept uncritically the proposition upon which Appleby immediately embarked.

'Good afternoon,' Appleby said. 'It's been a bit of fancy dress for everybody this afternoon, has it not? I wish I could get rid of mine as you seem to have got rid of yours. But I'm dressed up like this to amuse a friend. He's the real thing: the ruler of a fabulously wealthy state in the Middle East.'

'I don't hold with any of that sort.' The balloon man, as he supplied this information, treated Appleby to a glance of cautious and uncertain animosity.

'And he happens to be very interested in balloons. Would you say, now, that you're here at Drool Court on an amateur basis or on a professional one?'

'I'm not a bloody taxi, if that's what you mean.'

'It is what I mean, more or less. But you do undertake

something like what might be called chauffeur-driven private hire?'

'Funny man, are you?' The balloon man asked this question quite ferociously. 'I'm on a stupid enough job as it is. I'm supposed to go up, and while I'm still over this blasted place drop a lot of silly little envelopes that have something to do with a raffle. But nobody seems interested, so it's a bloody frost.'

'But at least you'll get your fee.'

'I'll get my fee, or see that Chitfield bastard a damn sight further.'

'Well, I have a slightly different proposition. You take up myself and this prince —'

'I don't hold with wogs.'

'He isn't a wog. He's the wealthiest and most powerful man in all Arabia.' Appleby was rather pleased with this. 'You take us up, and we sail away, and you come down again wherever you think proper. Only it must be more than five miles from Drool. My friend would insist on that.'

'How much?'

'One might appropriately say the sky's the limit. But better be precise. Fifty pounds down — I have that in a pocket under this idiotic get-up.' Appleby paused for a moment. 'And the remaining nine hundred and fifty more or less on demand after the trip.'

'No kidding?' The balloon man was obviously much shaken by this.

'Absolutely none. But you'll have to be nippy. So keep a look out for us. The prince isn't accustomed to be kept waiting.'

'At a cool thousand,' the balloon man said, 'I'm your pal for the rest of the day.' He spoke almost as if he had been sobered up by this sudden contact with high finance. But then he took a dive into his basket and produced what was certainly a half-empty bottle of gin. 'Have a swig on it, chum,' he asked hospitably.

'Later, perhaps,' Appleby said. 'And just keep off any

more of it yourself. They don't approve of alcohol in Arabia.'

And Sir John Appleby turned and walked composedly away.

XIX

But if Appleby was composed, he was wary as well. He still knew, he told himself, far too little precisely what was cooking at Drool Court. Somewhere in the crowd (unless, indeed, he had by now made off) there lurked somebody, whether himself Arab or not, who at least for a time had believed himself to have been successful in assassinating the Emir Hafrait. This person was almost certainly one of a gang. And there might conceivably be more gangs than one. There might be one gang simply set on killing the Emir, and another intent upon the more ticklish task of making a hostage of him. The Emir himself seemed to take it as a matter of course that he had one set of enemies here and another there.

It was true that, once a substantial body of police arrived and the carriage-way up to Drool Court had been declared free of hazard, getting Hafrait clear of the place and back to his own Embassy or whatever need not be all that risky. Pride had even talked about a bullet-proof car. But an unknown degree of difficulty here lay with the Emir himself. This was because he was, in fact, an excessively touchy chap. Or perhaps only an excessively political one. He was concerned, that was to say, to project an image which would be impaired if it became known that he had to be hustled around by a bunch of English rural policemen. It might be briefly expressed by saying that a princely hauteur made him a difficult fish to deal with.

At the moment Hafrait was presumably still within the house, together with its owner and the Chief Constable and Professor McIlwraith. And now there was the bizarre circumstance that the house was being gaped at by some two or three hundred persons awaiting the ridiculous mumbo-jumbo of the Basingstoke Druids. It was possible that Richard Chitfield had asserted himself sufficiently to call off the Perlustration, but it was equally possible that the druids were already in occupation of the dwelling, and that their ritual was about to begin.

Appleby (attired as he still was) felt it desirable to enter as unobtrusively as he could. This meant taking the route through the string of greenhouses and the monstrous conservatory beyond them. The druids were perhaps not interested in such vitreous excrescences. The Chief Constable (armed with his little automatic) might have decided to constitute the conservatory his last redoubt. Only it wasn't going to come to that. Appleby wondered how Tommy Pride was going to receive the news that the Emir Hafrait's departure from Drool Court was to be by hot-air balloon.

Given reasonable luck, that was to say. And for a start he now made a circumspect detour round the motley crowd sitting and standing in front of the house. It was a move that suddenly confronted him with a small group of persons who were rather ostentatiously holding themselves aloof from the current centre of interest. Here, in fact, were Richard Chitfield's son and two daughters, together with that foiled desert lover, Tibby Fancroft.

'Good heavens! Whatever has become of Robin Hood?' It was Cherry Chitfield who had recognized Appleby first.

'Sir John is going to annoy our poor father,' Mark Chitfield said, 'by stepping into Tibby's shoes and carrying you off on the back of a dromedary. There's no other possible explanation. Wouldn't you agree, Patty?'

'Mark, dear, will you ever stop being a fool?' The elder Miss Chitfield alone seemed to acknowledge that something not decently compatible with routine frivolity had taken place at Drool that afternoon – and indeed that there was rational cause to fear that further outrage of a similar sort might bob up at any moment.

'I certainly had this get-up from Tibby,' Appleby said briskly. 'But if anybody's going to be carried off it isn't me. Tibby, you must consent to be an unremarkable young Englishman for the rest of the day. Do you mind?'

'I do think it's a bit odd.' Tibby Fancroft appeared genuinely perplexed rather than offended. 'Did you really make me take off that stupid stuff because you wanted it for yourself, Sir John?'

'No, I didn't. It was as I said: making your apology to Mr Chitfield still togged up in it would have been a failure in tact. It was only later that I thought of nobbling it. But can anybody tell me if the druids have got going yet?'

'See for yourself,' Mark Chitfield said rather crossly. 'It's still pretty well broad daylight. But you can see them arsing around with torches and candles. There in the upper windows. If they set the place on fire I doubt whether the insurance people will stand for it. Not from somebody like our dear papa.'

Appleby had no difficulty in disregarding this last remark. If Richard Chitfield had really allowed the druids the sole occupancy of his abode, this almost certainly meant that he and his three companions were in the conservatory still. Or four companions, if they still had the company of the constable from the Panda car. He glanced at his watch. Accurate timing, he told himself, was going to be the whole thing.

So he walked on. But before he reached the old stable yard and the first of the greenhouses he met with a further encounter – and one of a more agitated sort. The constable from the Panda car was in fact sweating and out of breath. So much was this so that words failed him for a moment, and Appleby spoke first.

'Well met,' he said. 'Just lend me your whistle, will you?'

'Sir?'

'Your whistle. It's in a good cause.'

'Yes, sir.' Much perplexed, the constable unclipped the whistle from its lanyard, and handed it to Appleby. 'But I was to find you, sir, and get you back to that glass place. I've been hunting everywhere.'

'Well, here I am. So just what was your Chief Constable's order?'

'Just as I said, sir. To find you and let you know.'

'Let me know! Let me know what?'

'About the foreign gentleman, sir. He has just vanished. Into thin air, as they say.'

'Well, that's premature, to say the least. Has your reinforcement arrived yet?'

'Not yet, sir. But in five or ten minutes they should be here. After finding you, I was to go on and find them. To guide them here like, since they're coming through the woods.'

'So they are. Well, off you go, constable. And tell them not to hurry.'

'Sir!'

'Just that. You know who I am?'

'Yes, sir. Of course I know.'

'Then take it as an order, although a shockingly irregular one. I'll see you through any difficulty. But the order is precisely that. I want no massive uniformed police presence for at least a quarter of an hour. Law, yes – but order, not. Do you understand that?'

'No, sir – not one bit.'

'A very good reply. I like to meet a thoroughly reliable officer. Now off you go.'

The Range Rover was still parked in the old stable yard; its engine was gently ticking over; its owner was in the driving seat, and momentarily engaged in stuffing a pipe with tobacco.

'Not long now,' Appleby said. 'But I'm sorry to keep you hanging around.'

'Oh, not a bit. Actually, I've been having quite a useful

time, trying to decide whether the little fellows' – and Dr Gillam jerked a thumb towards the rear of his vehicle – 'can at all be detected as responding to that military band. It's a moot question, you know, whether any animals can distinguish one musical phrase from another, and react correspondingly. Did Orpheus charm snakes? We just don't know. But I expect you've seen those Saadia chaps in Egypt put up an uncommonly convincing turn with serpents. They tootle away in the minor key, and the snakes keep time to it in what one can't help feeling is a congruously melancholy way. But I mustn't detain you with that sort of thing at the moment, Sir John. Just when do I get the green light?'

'Within the next twenty minutes at the very most, I'd say. Only it won't be a light. I'm going to blow a whistle. And it will all be a bit tricky, you know. I'm sorry that circumstances don't permit of a rehearsal.'

'I've been turning it over, of course. In my mind, that is to say. And I think we'll bring it off – the little fellows and myself. Just a single blast on a whistle?'

'Yes, a single blast. And now I must get back inside again, and see how it goes with the druids. Have you had a glimpse of them, Dr Gillam?'

'One or two glimpses as I wandered round.'

'What do you think of them?'

'I don't believe many of them would recognize Avebury or Stonehenge if they woke up in the middle of it.'

'We are at one there,' Appleby said, and walked on.

In the big conservatory, and beside the imprisoned palm tree, Appleby found only Richard Chitfield and the Chief Constable. And he put the less important question first.

'Where's McIlwraith?'

'Taken himself off to join the crowd.' Colonel Pride made this reply. 'He said he didn't feel he could be of any further help to us. As none of the villains around the place seem to have it in for him as they have for the Emir, it's no doubt a discreet withdrawal from the limelight.'

'Well, that's rational, if not exactly heroic. But your constable has just told me that the Emir has vanished too – which is a different thing altogether. Have you hidden him away somewhere, or has he simply taken himself off? I'd put nothing beyond our friend Hafrait. But it would be uncommonly inconvenient.'

'I can't say I agree,' Richard Chitfield said. 'And it's what has happened. He has simply walked out on us too. And I'm bound to say I'd be glad never to set eyes on him again.'

'Do you mean to say' – Appleby sounded justly indignant – 'that the two of you simply let him give you a nod and walk away through these greenhouses?'

'It wasn't quite like that, John.' Colonel Pride spoke as if under a slight sense of injury. 'Chitfield had to decide about those blasted druids, and whether they should be let go ahead in the deserted house. As we still seem to be under some obligation to play the whole thing down, I advised him to let it go ahead. To cancel their turn would set everybody talking and mystery-mongering. So the two of us made our way to the front door, and contacted the Grace-to-Maleldil chap straight away, and told him to go right ahead. It was when we'd got back here from doing just that we found Hafrait had disappeared. Folded his tents like the Arabs, you might say, and silently stolen away.'

'Rather as *being* an Arab, my good Colonel. And here I am, back again.'

Very properly astonished, these three conferring persons swung round – to find themselves indeed confronted once more by the Emir Hafrait. He was standing beside the trunk of the palm tree, and to this he now gave an affectionate pat. And when he spoke it was at once apparent that some quite new mood possessed him.

'My dear friends,' he said, 'it is something I used to take

great pleasure in as a boy. I had our peasant lads teach me the technique of it. They themselves were for ever scrambling up the date palms, stuffing themselves with the things, and then scampering down again. And I am delighted to find that I have retained the art. It is not perhaps a very courtly accomplishment. But it solves our problem, does it not?'

'What the devil do you mean?' Colonel Pride considered this demand, and presumably decided that it, too, was on the uncourtly side. 'What the devil does Your Excellency mean?'

'Simply that up there, at the very crest of the tree, I am totally invisible from below. So there I can tuck myself away until those various disaffected people grow tired of hunting for me and take themselves off. It is true, Chitfield, that they may express their disappointment by burning down your house. But I do not think that fire can have much effect upon conservatories. And it will give me pleasure to pick up some other modest dwelling for you. They are constantly coming on the market. I hear of one or another friend of mine buying one almost every week. Wealthy as we have all become, we retain a taste for an unassuming way of life.'

'I for one,' Appleby said, 'would prefer to see Your Excellency in a more elevated situation. And I have made, indeed, a very simple arrangement to that effect.'

'Sir John, I have already said that I am your man.' The Emir, although he could only be described as in an unwontedly gamesome state of mind, said this with sudden seriousness. 'I will do anything you direct — provided it does not involve surrounding me with phalanxes of British policemen. And you, Colonel Pride, must forgive me this peculiarity. It derives from no disrespect for your constabulary. It is simply that it would become a matter for public jesting among my compatriots. And jesting is best confined to private occasions, such as the four of us enjoy now.'

After this regal graciousness, there was nothing more

to be said. Appleby looked at his watch, and then turned to Richard Chitfield.

'Your wife's Basingstoke friends,' he said, 'had begun their prowl through the house, starting at the top, not more than a few minutes before I joined you here by way of the greenhouses. Have you any idea how long they propose to take over the whole precious business?'

'Not more than twenty minutes. The fellow said it would take longer with the Asperges — whatever they may be. But I put my foot down. Twenty minutes at the outside, I said, and then they could take themselves off in the motor-coach they arrived in.'

'I've seen the coach. It has been parked somewhere inside your grounds, and it's waiting for them now.'

'And a thoroughly good riddance. I don't expect they'll hang around. My wife has made me have a ridiculously large cheque waiting for them. It's an idiotic business. I don't see any sense in it at all.'

'I don't know that I'm altogether sure of that. And now there's about ten minutes to go. Time for a little briefing, if I may put it that way. In five minutes I shall be returning to the old stable yard, in order to skirt round the back of the house, and so arrive at the west end of the terrace on the main front. The druids, I imagine, will aim at making a slow and impressive procession to their coach. When that has begun, I shall blow a whistle. If you hear no whistle, you will know that something has gone wrong, and you will stay put here. The whistle, Your Excellency, will, among other things, be your signal to follow my own route rapidly, so as to join me on the terrace. And you and Mr Chitfield, Tommy, must consider yourselves as a strategic reserve. But there's no reason why, a minute or two after the whistle, you shouldn't come round to the front of the house, and see what's doing. Just given a bit of luck, it's likely to be quite worth watching.'

XX

The military band at the west end of the terrace was packing up. There was quite a lot of bustle involved, and Appleby felt that for a minute or two he could station himself on the fringe of it without attracting undesirable attention. In any case, having abandoned Tibby Fancroft's dark glasses and let his head-dress fall back over his shoulders, he was likely to be adjudged a sheik only of the most Pring-like variety, who had a little wandered from the flock. He judged it unlikely that any of the unknown number of kidnappers, assassins, and potential assassins present in the large crowd now assembled would undergo the disturbing experience of recognizing in so harmless a figure an Englishman for long experienced in the detection and prevention of crime.

Mr Pring himself was sitting in the front row, with Joan of Arc (and her banner bearing the Cross of Lorraine) beside him. Several other pseudo-sheiks, whether harmless or murderously disposed, were also in evidence. Even from some way off, it was possible to detect that the majority of Mr Chitfield's guests were by now either tired, or bored, or both. So why they should thus linger as spectators of a singularly pointless ritual was a mystery not easily to be elucidated. One way and another, the afternoon had presumably involved them in the expenditure of a good deal of hard cash, and they were perhaps merely determined to have their money's worth to the end. It was also to be observed that, at this jaded late-afternoon hour, birds of a feather were tending to flock together in what must be an entirely unconscious and instinctive way. On the one hand the grotesques had managed to clump themselves: the Teddy bears, the deep-sea divers, the Mickey Mice and the circus clowns were ranged more or less side by side; on the other hand were clustered those whose imaginations had inclined rather to polished society in times past: periwigs and patches and powder, furbelows and knee-breeches, elegant swords and gold-buckled shoes – a whole *belle-assemblée* (as the dramatist Congreve has it) of coquettes and beaux. A little behind and apart from all these grotesque or polished persons stood the driver of the druids' coach and a little army of brawny and plainly sardonic plebeians whose job it would presently be to clear up the mess.

The Perlustration appeared now to be far advanced, since the torches and candles of the Basingstoke Druids were glimmering feebly through the windows of the ground-floor rooms. And the druids, as if conscious that this in itself was a little on the unimpressive or unentertaining side, had begun a species of outlandish chanting – or rather yowling – which perhaps indicated that the climax of their mysterious activity had been attained. It was certainly true that a certain degree of tension was building up; among the more impressionable of the female spectators in particular there were occasional exclamations of apprehension and even horror, rather as if there was a distinct possibility that some hideous sacrificial deed was about to be perpetrated before them.

And then – in a slow and sinister fashion – the main portals of Drool Court turned on their hinges, and there stepped over the threshold, side by side, two figures already familiar to Appleby: the Grace-to-Maleldil druid and the female druid bedecked with mistletoe. Both held their elbows and clasped hands before them beneath their voluminous robes, and moved down a flight of steps from the terrace at a sort of stately leisure which was by no means unimpressive in itself. Then all the other druids followed, similarly comporting themselves and similarly two by two.

And it was at this point that Appleby blew his whistle.

It was, in its setting, a startling sound – but not nearly so startling as what immediately succeeded. From one side of the assembled company there erupted volley upon volley of deafening rifle fire; upon the other, and from a source which few remained sufficiently composed to discern, there advanced what appeared to be a writhing sea of serpents. An observer of literary inclination might have felt that the well-kept lawns of Drool Court were thick swarming now with complicated monsters, head and tail, Scorpion and Asp, and *Amphisboena* dire, *Cerastes* horned, *Hydrus*, and *Ellops* drear. It was within nobody's comprehension that here was nothing more than a van-load of grass snakes, no doubt companioned by a few mildly dangerous indigenous English adders. And the very small minority of Mr Chitfield's guests who might have retained their senses before this spectacle were submerged beneath the panic of the majority by further deafening salvoes of musketry apparently coming nearer and nearer on the other flank. There could be no doubt of what was happening. The great Chitfield fête was ending in pervasive and discreditable panic.

And most panic-stricken of all were the Basingstoke Druids. The head of their procession was now about half-way to its coach, and its more resolute members were keeping up their yowling – if only with the deter-mination of despair, but sufficiently to contribute distin-guishably to the disordered noises alike of the unnerved mob which the spectators had become, and of a peculiarly savage yelling and cheering on the part of the still invisi-ble rude soldiery. For some moments the druids were of two minds. Those in the rear made indecisively to retreat to the house; those in front were for struggling on to their waiting coach. But only the coach conceivably offered effective escape, and soon they were all shoving and clawing their way ahead. Here and there, as a consequ-ence, bouts of fisticuffs between these priestly persons and the more enraged among the spectators broke out in a ragged but spirited fashion. And it was at this point that Appleby found the Emir Hafrait standing beside him.

'Thieves,' the Emir said composedly. 'Altogether, Sir John, a remarkable spectacle.'

This was undeniable. The struggling druids had perforce abandoned that curious box-like posture by which their arms had been held out in front of them beneath their ample robes, and as a consequence their path was marked by a trail of all the most superior knick-knackery in the Chitfield mansion. Some of it, being of the most delicate and precious porcelain, was doomed from the moment it fell. So, probably, was a number of small pictures collected during the Perlustration by those industrious but nefarious visitors. Among them – *horribile dictu* and *horresco referens* – was that work of art so admired by Tibby Fancroft, François Boucher's rosy and arsy-versy girl. But what chiefly bestrewed the sward was the Chitfield family silver, which might conceivably be recovered in no more than a slightly scratched and dented condition.

'Remarkable, indeed,' Appleby said. 'But not likely to distract your murderous compatriots for more than three or four minutes at the most. So we run.'

'Run!' exclaimed the Emir.

'Yes, run. And just follow me.'

And the Emir Hafrait ran.

The balloon was by now attracting no interest whatever, and was straining at its moorings as if anxious to see the last of a thoroughly unsatisfactory afternoon. At a first glance its proprietor himself (to whom Appleby had promised – strictly on behalf of the Emir – a taxi-fare of a thousand pounds) appeared to have deserted his post. But this was not so, since a shout brought his uncertainly swaying head and shoulders up from within the large basket-work affair which might be termed the passenger's accommodation provided by this kind of craft.

'*Two* shousand pounsh!' he now bellowed truculently. And to lend emphasis to this ultimatum, he picked up and brandished above his head a bottle which until lately had held a certain amount of gin.

'Drunk and incapable,' Appleby said to the Emir. 'So we must take the fellow's balloon by storm – you from the far side while I operate from here. He can't fend off both of us at once. So over the top, Your Excellency, and between us we'll chuck him out.'

This summary procedure went like clockwork, and within seconds the bemused aeronaut had been ejected from the basket and was attempting, but with no success, to get on his feet with sufficient security to contrive some further effective action. The speed with which so satisfactory a state of affairs had been achieved was just as well. For it was now possible to see that two figures had detached themselves from the continuing chaos in front of Drool Court, and were running towards the balloon with a purposiveness which reflected a good deal of credit on their ability to think rapidly on their feet.

'And now we are our own navigators,' Appleby said. 'And the initial moves I imagine to be easy enough. We simply cast off those two ropes or hawsers, chuck out a couple of bags of sand – and Your Excellency takes his leave of Mr Chitfield's unfortunate fête in a suitably elevated fashion. And just to think that I was lately considering the possibility of stuffing you into the boot of a car.'

The Emir took this last remark in good part, and proved remarkably adaptable to the needs of the moment. So they were airborne within seconds, and suffered no further immediate inconvenience than the passage, between them or beneath them, of a few revolver bullets discharged by the two baffled pursuers below. These elicited from the Emir what was presumably a malediction in his native tongue.

'I think,' Appleby said, 'that we are going to pass straight over the house, and with plenty of height to spare. And then there will be what is rather grandly called the Forest of Drool. It's quite a pleasant stretch of country for walking, but might be a little awkward to attempt a landing in. Ah! Things seem to be calming down beneath us.'

This was true. Richard Chitfield and Dr Gillam could be distinguished as standing together on the terrace – and Gillam was no doubt offering an appropriate apology for any inconvenience which a misfortune to his Range Rover had occasioned. The defenders of Mafeking, it occurred to Appleby, might momentarily be in severe disfavour, but Tommy Pride could be trusted to make it clear that they had in fact rendered signal assistance to the preserving of law and order. The coach of the Basingstoke Druids, now rapidly shrinking to the dimensions of a Dinky toy, remained where it had been, with its late occupants vainly clamouring round it: they would be picked up, no doubt, by the advancing posse of police.

'They've spotted us,' Appleby said.

This was true also: first in small groups, and then throughout the whole concourse, heads were being tilted back as their owners focused upon the object overhead. The Emir seemed to find this circumstance appropriate and agreeable.

'I am conscious,' he said, 'of having occasioned our friend Chitfield a good deal of inconvenience in the course of the afternoon. He cannot, indeed, be acquitted of a certain degree of injudicious behaviour, and in point of high policy and *raison d'état* his conference was of no value whatever. Nevertheless to him and his guests it will be proper to offer a courteous farewell.' Having said this, the Emir stood up somewhat hazardously on what appeared to be a sackful of sand, so that the greater part of his person was visible from below. Thus positioned, he raised both extended arms shoulder-high and let his open hands, each slightly cupped, gently rise and fall in air. It was a gesture, Appleby thought, papal rather than regal in suggestion; not the mere movement of the wrists with which royal personages in Britain can do much, but rather that repeated *sursum corda* motion whereby the Bishop of Rome exalts and edifies whole multitudes of the faithful.

Appleby himself took what was perhaps a more realistic view of the situation. He had never in his life gone for a ride in a balloon. And now, looking up at the underside of the gaily variegated fabic from which, with a gentle pendulum-like sensation, he and the Emir depended, he felt himself to be in a situation of the sort that wonderfully concentrates the mind. It all *looked* so easy, floating up and along like this. But how on earth did one control the thing? It couldn't be exactly complicated, since there seemed to be very little to be complicated with. So there must be all the more need for a bit of know-how about what there was.

'We have to remember,' Appleby said, 'that balloons of this sort are brilliantly coloured partly just for fun, but also so that they can be spotted from quite far off by anything that might get in their way.'

'Concorde, for example, Sir John. We must certainly avoid that.'

'But we also have to avoid any further rendezvous with your enemies down there. So, for the moment, it's all to the good that we're gaining altitude fairly rapidly. But the climb might become uncomfortable if it went on too long. I have an idea that the red lever on those controls is for going up rather than coming down, and that what it does is to start a most alarming burst of flame under the open mouth of the thing. It generates more hot air, and up you go.'

'And to come down?'

'Trickier, I rather think. It would, of course, come down eventually without our taking any action at all. But whether it would be over land or over the North Sea, I haven't a clue. We're certainly going almost due east now.'

'It is to be supposed that in some fashion one gently deflates the balloon.'

'Just so, Your Excellency. And it's my guess that the blue nylon cord so carefully secured over there operates what one might call a zip. But the manoeuvre is probably irreversible. So one would proceed with caution.'

'I am well accustomed, my dear Sir John, to delicate situations. Caution and prudence are not among the major virtues. Nevertheless, there are situations that demand them. Your career and mine, I judge, have in equal measure made us aware of that.'

Appleby (who was coming rather to like the Emir Hafrait) conjectured that this last remark had been of a complimentary nature, and he murmured an appropriate reply. But he then added a more forthright remark.

'I'd be uncommonly glad,' he said, 'to be sure we had a good dinner ahead of us.'

'Yes, indeed. And accompanied with a glass of champagne.' But this avowal seemed to perturb the Emir. 'That, my dear Sir John, is – as one says to the newspaper men – not for the record. The Prophet – praise be to his name – disapproved of music. Yet all Islam innocently indulges in it. The Prophet – praise be to his name – forbade the use of alcohol. But there, some of us at least a little slip up at times.'

'A matter of what Catholics call a venial sin.'

'Precisely so. How well we have come to understand one another, my dear Sir John.'

So the flight (if a balloon is to be described as in flight) continued. Drool Court and its demesnes had dipped over even an extended horizon some time ago. Woodland lay now beneath them, with here and there a glade across which trees cast long shadows thrown by the westering sun. And the balloon was by this time losing altitude. Appleby took no step to alter this. But he gave much attention to the terrain as it flowed on like a gigantic panorama on its cylinders below.

'I really think,' he said.

'I beg your pardon, Sir John?'

'I really think that a moment for action has arrived.'

And Appleby began, quite gently, to pull on the blue nylon cord.

So the balloon grounded, neatly if not altogether happily, in the middle of Lady Appleby's shrub roses. (There were to be a few survivors among the Fantin Latours, but the Nuits de Young proved annihilated for good.) The effect was as if some monstrous and garish bloom from science fiction's outer space had suddenly crashed down upon the carefully cultivated wild garden of Long Dream Manor. It was unlikely that Judith Appleby would be amused.

As for Sir John and the Emir Hafrait, they were considerably shaken, terra firma seeming to have suddenly surged upwards in a malign fashion and bruised them all over. Both were on their feet, however, before the aged Hoobin, disturbed in his second perusal of that morning's *Daily Mirror* in the gardener's shed, arrived on the devastated scene. Hoobin was accompanied by his nephew Solo – who, although yawning frequently, was at least half-awake.

'Furriners!' Hoobin said. 'Drat me if they ain't furriners.'

'Moon-folk,' Solo suggested. 'Dropped from one of them rockets.' And Solo, as if conscious of having indulged an unseemly loquacity, retreated hastily behind his uncle. But Hoobin was himself now alarmed. He had recognized his employer – who had left home earlier in the day dressed up as Robin Hood, and had now returned from the heavens swathed (like his companion) in what appeared to be a number of table-cloths, but which might well be cerements or grave-clothes too hastily wound around a Sir John Appleby mistakenly supposed to be dead.

'Hoobin,' Appleby said, 'there is nothing that can be

done about this at present. So take Solo away, and get back to that newspaper. And if Your Excellency feels up to eighty yards on foot after that thumping and drubbing, we'll make our way indoors and find my wife.'

It was thus, then, that Appleby and his guest exchanged Drool Court for Long Dream Manor. They were met in the hall by Lady Appleby, who had been conscious of brief but sinister noises in the garden, and was on her way to investigate their cause. Suddenly confronted by her husband and a stranger, both weirdly attired, she was only mildly surprised and not at all disconcerted – her husband's peculiar profession, now become a hobby, having not infrequently in one way or another invaded his domestic sanctities.

'My dear,' Appleby said, 'I have the honour of presenting you to His Excellency the Emir Hafrait.'

'How do you do?' Judith said – and firmly took the initiative in shaking hands. 'I hope you'll stay to dinner.'

'It will be a pleasure,' the Emir said, and the Applebys listened while he expanded upon this through several well-turned sentences.

'But then,' Appleby said, 'the Emir must unfortunately get back to town. After we've washed and brushed up, I'll make a telephone call or two about that.'

'It will add to your kindness,' the Emir said.

'By the way, I'm afraid there will be a bill from, or on behalf of, that balloon man. We did treat him a shade roughly, did we not?'

'That is undeniable, Sir John. But the experience – so novel, at least to me – will have been worth the money. And it will be politic to treat him as having been wholly cooperative. So he had better be given a decoration as well.'

FIND OUT MORE ABOUT
PENGUIN BOOKS

We publish the largest range of titles of any English language paper-back publisher. As well as novels, crime and science fiction, humour, biography and large-format illustrated books, Penguin series include *Pelican Books* (on the arts, sciences and current affairs), *Penguin Reference Books, Penguin Classics, Penguin Modern Classics, Penguin English Library, Penguin Handbooks* (on subjects from cookery and gardening to sport), and *Puffin Books* for children. Other series cover a wide variety of interests from poetry to crosswords, and there are also several newly formed series – *King Penguin, Penguin American Library, Penguin Lives and Letters* and *Penguin Travel Library*.

We are an international publishing house, but for copyright reasons not every Penguin title is available in every country. To find out more about the Penguins available in your country please write to our U.K. office – Dept EP, Penguin Books Ltd, Harmondsworth, Middlesex UB7 0DA – unless you live in one of the following areas:

In the U.S.A.: Dept DG, Penguin Books, 299 Murray Hill Parkway, East Rutherford, New Jersey 07073.

In Canada: Penguin Books Canada Ltd, 2801 John Street, Markham, Ontario L3R 1B4.

In Australia: Marketing Department, Penguin Books Australia Ltd, P.O. Box 257, Ringwood, Victoria 3134.

In New Zealand: Marketing Department, Penguin Books (N.Z.) Ltd, P.O. Box 4019, Auckland 10.

In India: Penguin Overseas Ltd, 706 Eros Apartments, 56 Nehru Place, New Delhi 110019.

Michael Innes in Penguins

LORD MULLION'S SECRET

Mullion Castle nestles in the heart of rural England, the country seat of Lord Mullion.

Charles Honeybath, RA, has been commissioned by Lord Mullion to paint the portrait of Lady Mullion. With his keen eye for facial features and his unerring nose for human motive, Honeybath perceives a peculiar state of affairs at the stately home.

And with Lady Camilla upstairs, old and infirm of mind, holding the key to the family's past and pecadilloes, the chances of discovering the truth are one in a – Mullion.

THE MICHAEL INNES OMNIBUS

Clues baffle and suspects abound in these exhilarating novels: *Death at the President's Lodging, Hamlet, Revenge!* and *The Daffodil Affair*. In them the literary touch of Inspector Appleby is called upon to tackle the macabre murder of a University President, the shooting of the Lord Chancellor while he was acting the part of Polonius, and the simultaneous disappearance of a half-witted girl from London and a half-witted horse from Harrogate.

'A master – he constructs a plot that twists and turns like an electric eel: it gives you shock upon shock and you cannot let go' – *The Times Literary Supplement*

THE AMPERSAND PAPERS

Strolling along a Cornish beach, Sir John Appleby narrowly escapes being hit by a falling body. Murder most foul. Or is it?

Michael Innes, the Master of the detective novel, here at his witty, stylish, gripping best.

THE GAY PHOENIX

It is not easy to step into your dead brother's shoes. Apart from the general fit, Arthur Povey discovers that his new role as maverick tycoon requires a more radical adjustment than he had ever foreseen. The confusions of a mismanaged financial empire force him into marriage, crime, attempted murder and despair at this change of fortune. His biggest mistake was to purchase a country estate that made him neighbour of that greatest of detectives, Sir John Appleby, erstwhile head of Scotland Yard.

and

APPLEBY'S END

AN AWKWARD LIE

THE BLOODY WOOD

CANDLESHOE

HONEYBATH'S HAVEN

Lionel Davidson in Penguins

THE CHELSEA MURDERS

Under the very noses of the police, and in tantalizing view of the reader, a psychopathic killer evades detection.

'Lionel Davidson restores a lost glitter to the detective story' – Matthew Coady in the *Guardian*

'An entertainment . . . A puzzle. A black comedy. A pleasure through and through' – H. R. F. Keating in *The Times*

Winner of the Crime Writers Association Gold Dagger Award

A LONG WAY TO SHILOH

A fragmented Scroll holds the key to the most ruthless treasure hunt of all time . . . Buried somewhere in Israel is the True Menorah, the great golden symbol of Judaism, lost for two thousand years. The Israelis have a copy of the Scroll, so do the Jordanians, who also have a ready supply of infiltrators and hit-men.

The Israelis have Caspar Laing, a brilliant young Professor of Semitics with a genius for code-cracking and a most un-academic libido . . .

'A very superior thriller indeed' – *Daily Mail*

Winner of the Crime Critics' Award for the Best Thriller of its Year

and

MAKING GOOD AGAIN

THE NIGHT OF WENCESLAS

THE ROSE OF TIBET

SMITH'S GAZELLE

THE SUN CHEMIST

THE WIDOW

'Van der Valk's widow, Arlette, steps into her dead husband's shoes, and trips over herself, irresistibly' – *Yorkshire Post*

After the death of her husband, Piet van der Valk, life gets boring for his widow, Arlette. So she chooses to remarry, a decision which spurs her into setting herself up as an advisory agency.

Clients, though, bring with them not merely their own problems but also danger and threats upon her own life . . .

The background is Strasbourg – a regional capital with unusual riches and resonance which attracts the best from both France and Germany. And it is into this city of crossroads that Nicolas Freeling launches the resourceful Arlette.

ONE DAMN THING AFTER ANOTHER

Nearly ten years after her husband's murder, Arlette is happily remarried to a phlegmatic Englishman and running a one-woman agency in Strasbourg which undertakes everything from detective investigation to the dispensing of tea and sympathy.

As she uncovers the activities of an illegal fur-trader, comforts an abandoned husband, undertakes a trip to the Argentine to retrieve a runaway delinquent, life for Arlette seems to be becoming just one damn thing after another.

And a cold voice threatening her on the telephone brings the last of Van der Valk's pigeons home to roost . . .

and

THE DRESDEN GREEN

GADGET

THE KING OF THE RAINY COUNTRY

A LONG SILENCE

THE NIGHT LORDS

WOLFNIGHT

CASTANG'S CITY

THE BLOOD OF AN ENGLISHMAN
James McClure

At first, it looked much like any other dead body – breathtaking in its own way, of course, but nothing special . . . Then he saw that the arm bones had been fractured by a knot, a knot that must have been tightened by a giant – or a human gorilla.

The celebrated detective team of Lieutenant Kramer and Sergeant Zondi are on the track of what appears to be a gigantic killer possessed of hideous strength. A murderer so out of the ordinary should be easy enough to find, yet to Kramer's intense embarrassment, he proves remarkably elusive.

LANDSCAPE WITH DEAD DONS
Robert Robinson

The wit and iconoclasm that we expect from the presenter of BBC Radio's *Stop the Week* abound in this malicious little academic exercise . . . For when the Vice-Chancellor is despatched among the statues with a dessert knife, the dreaming spires of Oxford are rudely awakened and all Hell is let loose. Caught with their trousers down (in front of the Ladies' Eight too!), the unlucky thirteen of Warlock College are given the third degree by Inspector Autumn of Scotland Yard, and all is revealed.

THE BOY WHO FOLLOWED RIPLEY
Patricia Highsmith

'The fourth in her saga about Tom Ripley, murderer, con-man, forger, coolly loving husband of Heloise, and squire of a pleasant estate in France. It is not so much what happens in these novels that gives them their power as the cold, detached writing which, one feels throughout, overlays a cauldron of intensity, violence and horror. Once I begin a novel by Miss Highsmith I am hypnotized' – Patrick Cosgrave in the *Daily Telegraph*

A MIND TO MURDER
P. D. James

A literary party is in sedate swing. Until Scotland Yard calls for the author. Not to sign an edition of his verse but to investigate a murder.

The Steen Psychiatric Clinic catered strictly for upper-class neuroses. But someone in that elegant institution had attempt-ed a total cure. In the basement record room sprawled the body of the Administration Assistant with a chisel through her heart. There were those who thought it inappropriate that a man who caught murderers should also write verse. However, Superintendent Adam Dalgliesh had a habit of confounding his critics. Even with Psyche as his Muse.

More Crime and Mystery in Penguins

THE MARGERY ALLINGHAM OMNIBUS

Whether he's faced with a deadly game of hide-and-seek in a remote Suffolk house, protecting a retired judge from assassination or an international ring of rather special art collectors, Albert Campion holds his own. His deceptively innocent appearance and mild manners mislead not a few in the three novels contained here: *The Crime at Black Dudley*, *Mystery Mile* and *Look to the Lady*.

'Always of the elect, Margery Allingham now towers above them' – *Observer*

THE NICOLAS FREELING OMNIBUS

Because of the Cats, *Gun Before Butter* and *Double-Barrel* – three gripping, high-tension thrillers are included here, and they all feature that most unorthodox detective, Van der Valk. Whether he is asked to investigate an unpleasant case of teenage violence, sent to solve a commonplace murder, or assigned to a dreary town to uncover the author of poison-pen letters, he always gets the cases no one else wants. Cool, amiable and incurably curious, he probes the routine surfaces . . . and finds himself in dangerous places.

'Van der Valk remains the most subtle, complex and interesting of fictional police detectives' – Edmund Crispin in the *Sunday Times*

More Crime and Mystery in Penguins

THE PENGUIN COMPLETE SHERLOCK HOLMES
Sir Arthur Conan Doyle

In four novels and fifty-six short stories, the exciting adventures of Baker Street's most famous resident, Sherlock Holmes. Known and loved by generation after generation, this shrewd amateur detective, with faithful Watson by his side, has earned his place in our national life and social history.

Containing

A STUDY IN SCARLET

THE SIGN OF FOUR

THE ADVENTURES OF SHERLOCK HOLMES

THE MEMOIRS OF SHERLOCK HOLMES

THE RETURN OF SHERLOCK HOLMES

THE HOUND OF THE BASKERVILLES

THE VALLEY OF FEAR

HIS LAST BOW

THE CASE-BOOK OF SHERLOCK HOLMES

More Crime and Mystery in Penguins

THE PENGUIN COMPLETE
FATHER BROWN
G. K. Chesterton

Forty-nine quietly sensational cases investigated by the high-priest of detective fiction, Father Brown.

Immortalized in these famous stories, G. K. Chesterton's little Norfolk priest has entertained and endeared himself to countless generations of readers. For, as his admirers know, Father Brown's cherubic face and unworldly simplicity, his glasses and his huge umbrella, disguise a quite uncanny understanding of the criminal mind at work . . .

Containing

THE INNOCENCE OF FATHER BROWN

THE WISDOM OF FATHER BROWN

THE INCREDULITY OF FATHER BROWN

THE SECRET OF FATHER BROWN

THE SCANDAL OF FATHER BROWN